# CARRY
# MY
# TEARS

## TO SHILOH

# CARRY MY TEARS

## TO SHILOH

Beverly R. Green

Ichthus *Publications* · Apollo, Pennsylvania

Our goal is to provide high-quality, thought-provoking books that foster encouragement and spiritual growth. For more information regarding Ichthus Publications, other IP books, or bulk purchases, visit us online or write to support@ichthuspublications.com.

*Printed in the United States of America*

ISBN: 978-1-946971-43-2

www.ichthuspublications.com

MANY THANKS

*to Mr. Patrick Lacher, my historical consultant. Your
information was invaluable!
Thank you to Mrs. Patricia Irwin, Mrs. Lynn Lacher, and
friends and family who continue to encourage me and pray
for me in my effort to carry the tears of the Master.
Thank you to Fish, Aaron, Jorja and Penni for "Stitch."
As always, to God be the glory!*

*Carry My Tears To Shiloh*

*is dedicated to my husband, my "warrior poet," Marty, who believes in me and the vision for my books.*

# Prologue

The April sky was clear and sunny, but the mountain breeze still carried the slightest chill as Johnny Maghee stood in the cemetery high on a hill behind the remains of his ancestor's house on Big Bear Mountain in the state of Tennessee. It was a small family cemetery surrounded by towering oak, maple and poplar trees. Many of the people buried in it had died in the 1800s. The names on the oldest stones had been weathered away, but some of the epigrams remained. Twelve-year-old Johnny found those epigrams fascinating. As he contemplated one of the epigrams, he heard someone approach from behind him. He knew without turning that it was his father.

"It says, 'CARRY MY TEARS.' What do think it means?"

"Well, Johnny, that's Caleb Maghee's grave. He was known for being the best preacher in this part of the country. They say literally thousands of people came to know the saving grace of Jesus because of this man's preaching. The legend is that he would labor on day and night helping people out wherever he could, and when anyone asked him why he worked so hard, he would tell them that the heart of Jesus broke for all human suffering and that Jesus Himself had instructed him to carry His tears to a lost and dying world."

"Dad, do you believe Jesus really talked to him, you know, like I'm talking to you?"

"I don't rightly know, but I do know that many a soul is in heaven now because Caleb believed He did."

# Brothers

The summer of 1850 brought blistering hot days, even on Big Bear Mountain. The air did not move, and from the trees there was not even a whisper of leaves. Even the birds were quiet, as if they, too, thought that it was too hot to be out and about and so had taken to their nests under thick leaves. The brilliance of the afternoon sun washed out the color of the grass and leaves. For the most part, the world dozed while it waited for the brutal heat to pass; however, there rose one spark of activity from an ideally located lake below a log house where lived the family Maghee.

What could be heard were voices. Two skinny, dark-haired, dark-eyed boys laughed and yelled to one another as they tried to catch fish by hand. The cool, blue mountain lake in which they swam hosted a great many fish, mostly small sunfish and crappie that huddled in the cattails and reeds growing along the water's edge. There were also "cats" that fed along the bottom, some grown quite large. The boys, aged five and seven, were already expert swimmers and divers and could often come up with a slippery captive in hand, although holding on to it once it was caught was more difficult. The challenge was the best part though, and a perfect way to spend a hot afternoon.

Their grandfather fished further around the lake. Abel Maghee was after the more elusive bass which also lived in the lake. Every once in a while, a dragonfly would venture out over the open water, and in a great feat of propulsion, a huge bass would emerge and capture the unfortunate dragonfly in its large mouth, seem to hover in the air for a moment, and then reenter the lake with a splash. The grandfather would smile and tip his hat to the large fish and promise in his slow drawl, "One day, Mista Bass, one day . . ."

Suddenly, that peaceful scene was interrupted by a literal howl from the older boy. He thrashed in the water, went under, which changed his howl to a frightening "blub, blub, blub, blub," and came to the surface again resuming the howl.

Abel dropped his pole and headed in the direction of the boys, the younger of whom began to scream out of sheer fright. "What in tar-nation . . . ?" he muttered as he rushed to the aid of his grandson fairly quickly for a man of his age.

The boy had exited the lake by the time Abel got to him. He was still jumping and yelling and spinning in circles on one foot. "Caleb!" the old man shouted to get him to stop. "I cain't hep ye if yur spinnin' like a tornadie!" He took him by the arm and the boy stopped jumping, but bent double in pain. Then Abel could see the cause of the uproar: a snapping turtle had attached itself to the boy's big toe and was hanging on tenaciously through all the gyrations. Its tiny mouth, for it was a very small turtle, was just enough to pinch down on the boy's toe and hold firm.

The boy, Caleb, dropped down on the ground whimpering, "Git it off, Grampaw! Please git it off!" Abel grabbed a stick off the ground and began to poke at the turtle. The turtle, with impressive ferocity for a little tike, let go of the toe and attacked the stick. Caleb was free, but with a pinched and bloody toe which he agilely stuck in his mouth in an attempt to ease the throbbing pain. Abel threw the stick, turtle and all, far out into the water. When the smaller boy, Jacob, saw that, he raced out of the water for all he was worth to avoid his own encounter with the aggressive reptile.

"Why'd you throw 'im back in the lake, Grampaw?" Jacob asked.

"He'll make good soup one day. Caleb can ketch 'im agin in a coupl'a years."

"Oh no, I won't!" Caleb blurted. Abel laughed a quiet "Humph, humph, humph." Jacob joined him and began to mimic Caleb's "turtle dance." Caleb finally saw the humor and laughed as well, as his grandfather tied a large bandage made from his handkerchief around the offended toe. That evening, Caleb proudly displayed his bandaged toe to his maw and paw.

"In a few years I'm gonna ketch that ol' boy and Maw can make a big pot a' soup!"

From that day on, Caleb was called *Turtle* by his family and anyone else who sat still long enough to hear the story, and with every telling, that turtle got bigger and bigger, but regardless of how big he got in their minds, the fear of him did not keep those boys out of the lake, although it might have made them more careful. For a while, feeling a little left out and wanting to be just like his big brother, Jacob insisted on being called *Little Turtle*, but Caleb would retort, "You ain't no turtle, Jake! Yer just a tadpole." So Jacob became *Tadpole*, often shortened to just *Tad*, and by the time the boys were back in school in the fall, those were the names by which they were known.

# Life on Big Bear

Seasons came and went with comfortable predictability at the Maghee farm on Big Bear Mountain. In the summer, Turtle and Tadpole still swam, caught salamanders along the edge of the lake, and fished with Abel, but their chores became more rigorous and time-consuming. The corn fields below their large, rustic log house needed tending, the cow and goats needed milking, roofs and fences needed mending, the vegetable garden needed weeding, and the mules and chickens needed feeding and care. By the ages of ten and twelve, Turtle and Tadpole were already doing a grown man's share of the work. There were only three adults: Abel, his son who was named for him but called Abe, and Abe's wife Alice, plus the two boys to make sure the farm ran well. One thing was sure, there was no time to be bored. Life was not easy, but they ate well, worked well, and played well, and at night, they slept very well.

In the fall, the boys were still allowed to attend school except for the days when they were needed to help with the harvesting of the corn. Many boys and girls their age could not go further than first or second grade, where they learned their letters and numbers and how to write their names, because they were needed at home. Turtle and Tadpole's parents, though, scraped and sacrificed and sometimes hired on a little help so the boys could get as much education as possible. Turtle Maghee had reached the seventh grade, the highest achievement offered in Big Bear Creek School, and for this he was a local hero. Not only was he the oldest and most accomplished student in the school, but he was also more educated than anyone else in the whole Big Bear community other than Mr. Adams, the schoolmaster. If anyone ever needed a letter or contract written, they called Turtle; if they needed a document read and explained, they called Turtle. They were willing to pay him what they could—a coin, a chicken, a bag of turnips—and so Turtle contributed to the family income. Turtle enjoyed reading and learning and helping the younger children to learn, and Mr. Adams often remarked that Turtle was a born teacher and an accomplished writer. In fact, Turtle often entertained the idea of going off to Nashville or Memphis one day to apprentice at a newspaper and to become an important writer who informed the public of great events. Tad sometimes felt a twinge of jealousy over his brother's notoriety, but he pushed those feelings deep down inside. He was proud of his big brother, as were his parents.

Tadpole did not care for school nearly as much as he cared for the three-mile-long hike down the mountain every morning and back up the mountain in the afternoon. He loved to be outside. His favorite fall pastime was hunting. At ten, Tad had only been able to finish his third grade work, but he was an

16

excellent marksman. He had already brought home turkeys, deer, rabbits, squirrels, ducks and quail for the family to eat. Turtle did all right with the big targets, but he fancied himself a writer, not a hunter, and it was Tad who brought in more meat even than his father and grandfather.

Fall was breath-taking on Big Bear Mountain. Bright orange, red and gold leaves exploded into a turquoise blue sky, yellow and purple wild flowers crowded into the road, and deep green fir and spruce trees cooled the fiery landscape. The crisp, clean air was full of the scents of smoke from home fires, tart apples and pears from the general store, and fresh cut hay from the fields. Silver frost tipped the tall corn stalks and glazed the amber pumpkins. During the early fall, workers were always out from dawn until dusk to bring in the abundance of the fields so there would be food on hand for a whole year. The land on Big Bear Mountain and down in the hollow of Big Bear Creek seemed almost supernaturally blessed year after year as the cornucopia of crops came in.

After harvest time, there was always a fair at Big Bear Creek. Plump livestock, colorful quilts, embroidery, breads, cheeses, and various preserves were brought for sampling, trading, and judging. Alice's pies consistently won blue ribbons and Tad consistently brought in the "big buck." Abel's favorite was the whiskey-tasting. For most of the year, he did not partake, having nearly died due to drink once—he had imbibed quite a bit, and in his state of inebriation, he tried to strike up a conversation with the wrong end of a mule who kicked him in the head and left him comatose for nearly a week, the scar forever visible in the middle of his forehead and his vision impaired—but during the fair he allowed himself to enjoy the various mixtures of excellent Tennessee corn whiskey. When he decided which one was best, he would drop a hint to his son and daughter-in-law, and that is what he would receive for Christmas—one bottle only to last the year. Turtle and Abe enjoyed competing in games of horseshoes and checkers, then walking at their leisure around the fairgrounds and talking to people they knew and did not see often. Everyone enjoyed the magnificent food and the hiatus from the normal heavy load of chores.

Soon after the fair came the cold weather and preparations for Christmas, always a joyous time that included a tree strung with popcorn and berries and hung with various trinkets the family had collected over the years. Except for Abel's whiskey, most of the Christmas gifts were homemade, but the day would not have been better if the gifts had been purchased from the finest store in Nashville. In 1853, Turtle and Tad worked all year after Turtle came up with the idea to make their maw and paw a miniature wooden stable with baked clay figures of Mary, Joseph, and the baby Jesus, along with a couple of animals and real hay on the stable floor. Unbeknownst to the boys, their grandfather had discovered their plan and carved a beautiful angel, painted her blue, and fashioned wings from the molted gray-white feathers of  doves that lived in the barn. Those gifts touched Alice so much that she cried, and even though Abe didn't say much, when it was time to put them away after the holiday, he wrapped every piece carefully in clean scraps of fabric and placed them in a wooden crate so they would be perfectly safe until the next Christmas rolled around.

That same year, Abel presented the boys with a very special gift, as well: a small, tawny, short-haired, pit bull-mix puppy. He seemed all eyes and paws when Abel brought him in from the barn where he had been hidden in a hay-lined box. Tad reached up to receive him as soon as he saw him in his grandfather's arms, and the warm, sleepy bundle became animated in a moment at the excited shrieks of the boys. Alice was in the process of lecturing them about being responsible for the dog when he jumped out of Tad's arms and raced across the floor directly into Alice's sewing basket, tumbling its contents onto the floor and running back to Tad with a look of extreme panic on his face.

The puppy whimpered as Tad picked him up to comfort him, but Turtle saw something. "Be careful, Tad! Look!" There was a needle stuck in the little creature's paw.

Alice, who wanted to be cross about the situation but just couldn't, calmly reached for the puppy's paw and gently pulled out the needle saying, "No stitches for you today, Darlin'." Only a tiny spot of blood rose from the needle's prick, and she wiped it with her apron.

Turtle petted the puppy and repeated, "No, sir, you don't need a stitch."

"That's a good name for ye, boy," Tad spoke softly to the puppy. "How 'bout it, Turtle? We kin call 'im Stitch."

"Stitch is a fine name," Turtle smiled at his younger brother.

"Yep, a mighty fine name," Abel agreed.

From that day on, Stitch shared in all the adventures of the boys, but he seemed to enjoy hunting with Tad best of all.

Winters were the family's quiet times when they became reacquainted with one another. Although the animals still had to be cared for, the house kept, and the meals cooked, and although school was still in session when the snow was not too deep to walk to town, there was time in the early darkness to sit together in the keeping room—a warm pine-log room just off the kitchen with a large and colorful braided rug, several chairs including a rocking chair where the boys had been comforted as infants, and where in those days, Alice did her mending and knitting.  It was the perfect place to tell stories and sing songs (accompanied by Abel's guitar) and to catch up on all the news from the papers that had accumulated during busier times of the year. It was during those quiet, dark evenings when the snow fell thick on the mountain that Abe and Abel competed at checkers, Tad taught Stitch how to do tricks like shaking hands and rolling over, and Turtle read to the family from newspapers and old story books, and last thing every night, from the Bible.

Then suddenly, a morning would dawn when it seemed that overnight the world awakened—the snow melted, tiny yellow-green leaves appeared on the trees and green shoots emerged from the ground, fiddleheads appeared in the woods and the black bears were spotted in the distance across the meadowlands. The first hints of spring announced the time to plow and plant and start the process once again. It also meant that a large wash tub would be brought out into the yard and filled with water warmed on the fire so baths could begin again.

The first bath of the spring was, in a word, liberating. After months of washing with a basin on a stand and tepid water from a pitcher, being able to immerse the whole body was heavenly. After Turtle read a newspaper article to the family about scented British soap, Alice decided to begin supplementing her homemade soap with fragrant herbs from her garden. The result was an odd combination of harsh ash and animal fat smells coupled with essences of basil, rosemary and mint—very luxurious. Alice always got the first clean tub, then the rest of the family would take turns in order of age, all the way down to Stitch. In reality, by the time Tad got his turn he would have come cleaner washing in the lake; however, the early spring lake water was still as cold as a witch's fingers in a brass jar, so the decision went for the tub.

Big Bear Mountain was like a little slice of heaven, and the Maghee family considered themselves blessed to live there.

# Camp Meeting

One evening in the spring of '55, after dinner was eaten, table cleaned up, and regular chores finished, Alice went to the loose floor boards behind the stairs, carefully lifted a couple of the boards, and removed a shiny, wooden box. She opened it and gently unwrapped several sets of silver spoons and forks. They were shiny but had a dark film covering them.

"Maw, what are those fer?" Tad was curious.

"Well, it seems next week there's goin' to be a camp meetin' at Big Bear Creek, and the preacher, Emmanuel Potter, is goin' to stay here with us," she smiled, "so I'm takin' out the fine things."

The words *camp meetin'* grabbed Turtle's attention and he also went over to see what Alice was doing. She had gathered salt, baking soda, a bowl of very hot water, and some rags. With the salt, soda, and a little of the water, she made a paste, and with one of the rags she applied it to a spoon and rubbed and rubbed. As she did, the dark, filmy tarnish began to come off. It was replaced by gleaming silver.

"Looky there, Turtle," Tad was in awe. "We're rich! We got us a honest-to-goodness treasure!"

Alice laughed her light, youthful laugh. "I don't know 'bout bein' rich, but this is the silver that was passed to yer daddy and me by my maw and paw on our weddin' day. It don't all match and one of the forks's got a bent prong, but don't it polish up purdy?" She held out the spoon she was working on. The bowl had begun to gleam and shine. "This silver is just like people, ya know?" She saw one of her teaching moments coming.

"Whaddaya mean, Maw?" Tad was willing to hear it.

"Sometimes people look a little rough and not too purdy on the outside. They get exposed to things around 'em that turn 'em that way, bad things they cain't control, just like things in the air around us tarnish up this silver; but if ya take a little time with 'em and find out what's under the tarnish, ye can find what's beautiful in 'em."

"I bet Jesus said that!"

"No, not Jesus," Turtle corrected his brother. Then he quoted something he remembered from his Bible reading: "I'll bring 'em into the fire; I'll refine 'em like silver and test 'em like gold. They'll call on my name and I'll answer 'em."

Alice smiled, "My little preacher-man."

"I ain't no preacher-man!" Turtle said and walked away.

*   *   *

Camp meeting was the second most exciting public gathering after the fair at Big Bear Creek. There was, of course, an active church in Big Bear. It was a small, white-washed building with plank floors and walls, a rough-cut lectern in the front, a stove for warmth in the winter, and a dozen long, very rustic benches without backs for the congregation to sit on. A steeple rose from the roof, but there was no bell in it. The front lawn sloped gently down to Big Bear Creek, which rushed and bubbled, playing the music of heaven all the way to the Tennessee River. Behind the building where the elevation was higher was a very old community cemetery where ghosts of the Blue Ridge walked in the moonlight according to the local children.

Since the community was so tiny, there was not a regular pastor to preach every week. One Sunday a month, the itinerant Preacher Nettles would come by to share a message. The other three Sundays, the pulpit would be filled by church elders who were willing to give a lesson from the scriptures, whether or not they could actually read those scriptures. Sometimes Abel preached, and when he did, everyone was sure to be in the meeting for a long time because Abel loved to talk, but since he was always so up-beat and positive, no one minded too much. Sometimes, elderly Brother Hugh would bring the Word, but he usually fell asleep at the lectern, standing up, right in the middle of his delivery. Once he even started to snore. What kept him on his feet in those moments no one knew, but it was suspected that the Holy Ghost Himself sent an angel to prop him up to keep him from falling and being injured. Brother Edwards occupied the sacred desk often. He claimed to be kin to the more famous Brother Edwards who, a century earlier, had preached such eloquent sermons about how all men dangled by a thread over the open mouth of hell. Women had been known to faint and men to run for the door during some of the elder Brother Edwards's more powerful messages, and Big Bear's Brother Edwards did his best to continue the famous preacher's reputation. For the most part, the combined wisdom of those men supplied the spiritual meals for Big Bear as the faithful congregation gathered every Sunday in the little building that served as church, courtroom and meeting hall.

However, once every spring a preacher would come to visit the small mountain community, and all the people from miles around would come to the meetings every night for a whole week. Families would provide wagon loads of food, cut logs to make benches, and practice music for the praise and worship. A home in the host community would be chosen to "put up" the preacher for the duration of the meeting—a very great honor. That year the Maghees were the chosen home.

For the next several days every moment that could be spared from farm chores went into preparation for the camp meeting. The level of excitement rose in anticipation of the words of Emmanuel Potter, a real preacher who had studied theology in a college up North.

The day finally came when a wagon pulled by two mules arrived in Big Bear Creek bringing three gentlemen. Two of the men, Hardy and Joe, were very large and muscular, fair of skin and hair, and soft in speech, while the third, Manny, was older, a good bit smaller, and a big bit more vocal. The three men and many Big Bear helpers cut the grass field for the meals on the grounds. They placed tables with benches around the field and up to the very border of the church cemetery to hold the food to be served before and after each meeting, the best part of the week according to some. They cleaned the little church until it was spotless.

As the work progressed, the three men gained the approval of the community. The two larger men were very hard-working, nice-looking, and quiet; however, Manny rapidly became the most popular with everyone (except the young, single women). Manny had wavy, brown hair that was beginning to show some signs of gray at the temples and that framed a still boyish face. He had the most astonishing green eyes that could crease in humor one moment and pierce the depths of a soul the next. He talked a lot, smiled a lot, and praised the Lord a lot. Every time one phase of the preparation was complete, he lifted his hands to heaven and shouted, "Praise the Lord!" When someone came up and introduced himself or herself, Manny's response was, "Good to meet you; praise the Lord!" followed by a warm handshake. The biggest "Praise the Lord!" came as the women began to arrive with pots and bowls and pans and trays of the best food Big Bear Creek and its surrounding area could produce.

Turtle and Tad loved being involved in any Big Bear Creek hubbub and so were very present at the preparation for camp meeting. They worked hard getting extra benches set up in the meeting house, and their diligence caught the attention of Manny who asked them their names. When they responded with the nicknames to which they had become accustomed, Manny laughed out loud and insisted on hearing how they happened to be labeled so. He laughed even harder at the story of the little snapping turtle bite, wiping tears of mirth from his eyes and responding, "Well, praise the Lord!" Stitch liked Manny, too, and followed him around to beg for an extra pet or scratch behind the ears. When it was time to eat, the boys looked around for Manny so they could introduce him to some of their mother's excellent pies, but he had mysteriously disappeared completely from the scene. They were getting concerned about him when people began to migrate into the church to find a seat. Hardy and Joe, who had been greeting people at the church entrance waved the boys in.

"Where's Manny?" Tad insisted.

"He'll be here soon. Hurry up and find a seat now," was Hardy's response.

"Where's the preacher-man?" was Turtle's question, as his eyes scanned the area for the dark-suited, sober, Bible-toting, intellectual he imagined Emmanuel Potter to be.

The boys jostled their way to the front and found a space to sit amidst the other children. Then Abel with his guitar, and several other musicians, two with fiddles and one with a harmonica, and four singers, commanded the attention of the crowd as they began to play and sing, "I got a home in glory!" The crowd joined in, singing, clapping their hands, and shouting "Amen!" and "Glory to Gawd!" Then slowly, Granny Campbell made her way to the front. She danced a halting dance, then began to spin in a slow circle, which gradually got faster. She flung her arms out wide and spun faster yet. The children exchanged glances. This is what they had been waiting for. Granny Flora and Granny Elma joined Granny Campbell, and all three spun around with arms wide and wailing at the top of their lungs, "Hal-le-lu-yer!" as long, gray, braided hair fell cascading down their shoulders in a rain of lace caps and hair pins. Suddenly, they took off in a victory march down the aisle of the church and out the door. Others fell in behind them until anyone who was able was circling the church in a Jericho march. The children, seeing their chance, began to run around the outside of the building, as well. What a commotion! Eventually, Granny Campbell danced back through the door and sank down on a bench. Several of the women went with her to prop her up and fan her with their aprons. The other grannies followed, and the furor deescalated from there. Before long, miraculously, everyone was seated again, panting, faces glowing from sweat and the great Presence.

Abel came forward and dismissed the rest of the musicians who had continued to play during this outpouring of spiritual energy. He cleared his throat and held up one hand to gain the attention of the crowd. "Brothers and Sisters," he began. "What a bountiful blessin' the Holy Ghost has laid upon us already in this here camp meetin'."

There were shouts of "Amen!" and "Hallelujer!" in response.

Abel raised his hands to quiet the crowd. A hush fell and a smile crossed the face of the old man. He was enjoying himself immensely! "Jus' like it says in the Good Book, 'Do not neglect to assemble yourselfs together, but exhort one another as ya see the great day approachin' (several enthusiastic *amens*). So we do like we're told, an' assemble today and ever day for the next week. And friends, it don't matter what ye come here a-seekin', the Lawd already knows what it is. The important thing is, ye come a-seekin' it, and Gawwwwd is merciful to provide!"

The *amens* were winding down, but Abel was not.

"Y'all know," he continued, "what a great and rare occasion it is when we are able to have a real, live preacher-man right here in Big Bear. One o' these days, it is our hope and prayer, to have a pastor of our own to preach ever Sabbath day (murmurs of agreement), but fo' now, the good Lawd has seen fit to send us a bless-ed man o' the cloth; a man who has studied the bless-ed word o' Gawd in college, no less; a man who travels all over the country to bring Gawd's blessin' in the form of powwwwerful words . . ."

The crowd was getting restless.

"C'mon Abel!"

"Let's get on with it!"

". . . a man after Gawd's own heart bringin' us a message from the throne room— the Rever'n' Emmanuel Potter!"

The man who walked up to the lectern to the applause of the people with his dark hair slicked back and dressed in a black suit with a white shirt and stove-top hat and a Bible under his arm was no other than Manny! The boys exchanged glances, amazed. Their new friend was the famous preacher!

"Praise the Lord!" the reverend opened, and the crowd once again erupted with enthusiasm. "The great English playwright William Shakespeare asked the question, 'What's in a name?' We are known to the people around us by a name.

Sometimes it's the name our mothers and fathers gave us, and sometimes we're known by something different. Today we're going to talk about what's in your name, praise the Lord, and I think you'll find it's more important than you thought."

Emmanuel Potter went on to talk about how God Himself had named some people, like Adam and Eve, and how He changed the names of some people, like Abram, Sarai, Jacob, Esther, Simon and Saul. He ended up in the book of Revelation from which he quoted:

"'He that hath an ear, let him hear what the Spirit saith unto the churches: to him that overcometh, I will give to eat of the hidden manna, and will give him a white stone, and in that stone a new name written, that no man knoweth saving he that receiveth it. And I saw the dead, small and great, stand before God; and the books of the dead were opened: and another book was opened, which is the book of life: and the dead were judged out of those things which were written in the books, according to their works. And death and hell were cast into the lake of fire. This is the second death. And whosoever was not found written in the book of life was cast into the lake of fire.'

"My friends, it doesn't matter what your name is, or whether you're known by Caleb or Turtle (laughter), or Jacob or Tadpole (more laughter), confess your sins and call on the name of the Lord. Yes, call on the name of Jesus, and your name will be written down in the Lamb's Book of Life."

Turtle watched as many people, young and old, men and women, the healthy and infirm, made their way to the make-shift altar that evening. Some cried and some shouted, and it seemed some walked away just as they came. Something in Turtle's young mind wanted to ponder all that, but then he remembered the food that was still piled high on tables in the fresh air outside, and he turned and walked out, headed for the pies.

That night, after the family had returned to the mountain and most of them had gone to bed, stomachs and souls filled to the bursting, Turtle sat with Stitch on a large rock below the house overlooking the lake. A full moon glowed and all the bright stars fairly twinkled in the heavens. There was a nip in the air, and the pregnant scent of spring was heavy and promising. The night was perfect, but Turtle's heart was not peaceful. He heard footsteps close behind him, and the preacher, who now looked like Manny again, mounted the rock and sat beside him.

"You sure have a lovely place here," Manny began and he scratched Stitch behind the ears, "and I'll bet this is your favorite spot."

"Sometimes. I like to come here to think." Turtle wanted to ask a question but he wasn't sure how to begin.

"It's a good thinking place, for sure."

"Manny . . . ?"

"Yes, Turtle."

"Um, is it okay if I still call you *Manny*, seeing as how you're the preacher and all."

"Of course it is, Turtle, praise the Lord! That's still my name. It's just a shortened version; one I save for my friends."

Both gazed out at the lake in silence for a while.

"Manny," Turtle tried again, "how can I know if my name is written in the Lamb's Book in heaven?"

Manny smiled. "Son, that's one of the easiest things and one of the hardest things in the whole world."

Turtle looked up into the preacher's face. No, he wasn't joking. "Wh-what does that mean?"

The preacher's voice was quiet and kind, and a little sad. "Well, it's like this. A lot of people want to spend a lot of time doing things to earn their way into the Book. They do a lot of good deeds and give away a lot of good things. They stop drinking, cussing and gambling. They come to camp meetings and church when they can, they help the hungry and homeless, and they read the Bible *if* they can. And then they spend a lot of time worrying about whether or not they're going to heaven. You understand?"

Turtle nodded his head. He really did understand.

"But there is only one thing a person can do. 'If you confess with your mouth the Lord Jesus Christ and believe in your heart that God raised Him from the dead, you will be saved.' So first you have to hear about it—that's my job—and then you have to believe it and confess it—that's your job. Sometimes we need help to believe, and that's all right. God understands. We just need to ask. Sometimes we don't have fancy words, and that's all right. We don't need them. You see, it would be the most unfair thing in the world if the rule was 'good people go to heaven and bad people go to hell,' because there's no measuring stick for good and bad. That's why the Bible says, 'For by grace ye are saved through faith; and that not of yourselves: it is the gift of God: not of works, lest any man should boast.' When we believe in Jesus and His sacrifice for us, that He died on the cross and took the punishment for all our sins, then we want to tell others about Him and we want to do good things out of a grateful heart, not because we are trying to earn His favor. See how that moon is reflected down there in the lake? Looks just the same as it does in the sky, right? Well, just like the perfect image of the moon up there is reflected in the lake down here, we want to be the image and likeness of Jesus, doing like He did, and He did good things and helped people. It becomes the way we live, but not what gets our names written down in the Lamb's Book of Life. Do you understand, Son?"

"I think so," Turtle responded, and he did understand the preacher's words, but the whole concept just seemed too wonderful and strange, and he was tired.

The two sat for a while longer in silence, contemplating something that was bigger and more astonishingly beautiful than even the full moon on the lake.

Finally, Turtle got up. "I think I'm gonna go to bed now, Manny. Hope you sleep well, Sir."

"Think I'll just stay out here a little longer. Sleep well, Son." Stitch accompanied Turtle as far as the door, then jogged back down to the rock by the lake.

Turtle entered the house to silence. The air seemed warm and stuffy after the chilly freshness of the outdoors. He plopped down next to Tad on the pallet prepared in front of the dying embers in the fireplace. They had given up their bed for the preacher. As he drifted off to sleep, Turtle mouthed the words silently, "Lord, help me believe."

In the middle of the night, Turtle awoke with a start. He had heard the preacher's voice whispering close to his ear, but when he opened his eyes, no one was there except a sleeping Tad, who was, in fact, snoring. Moonlight was pouring in and Turtle got up and walked to the window. He glanced into the face of the round, solemn moon and then down the hill toward the lake. In the clear, silver light, he could see Emmanuel Potter and Stitch still sitting on the rock.

# Jobie

Dawn came in a bustle. Corn cakes were mixed and put on the griddle. Thick cut bacon sizzled in a pan. A wedge of cheese was cut. A pot of coffee boiled. Alice was a whirl of skirt and apron, but she was in her element, and she smiled and hummed a tune, pausing briefly to call out, "Turtle, go milk the cow! Tad, roll up that pallet and fetch me the butter and maple syrup! Then come set the table!" The clatter of dishes and cups and bowls joined the cooking sounds as Turtle returned with the milk, just ahead of Abel, Abe, Manny, and a little Negro boy.

They all seated themselves around the table. Abe announced, "This here is Jobie. Found him walkin' through the corn field this mornin'. Said he was lookin' for work. I reckon we can use the help. Make him welcome."

In truth, what happened was that Abe caught Jobie stealing corn. Being a very understanding sort and assuming he was on the run and hungry, Abe "offered him a job" for room and board until another safe solution to the boy's dilemma might be found. Stitch walked slowly over to Jobie, sniffed him, and offered him a paw to shake. "Guess it's official then," Abe responded, and they all sat down to table.

Abel usually opened the meal with prayer, but this time he asked Manny to do the honors. "Praise the Lord!" was his answer and he prayed, "Father in heaven, I thank you for this family that has been willing to take in strangers and offer hospitality. Bless them, Lord, from Your great bounty and bless this food to give us strength to do Your will. Amen."

Everyone responded with "Amen!" and breakfast commenced. Abe then reminded them that chores had to be done before they left for camp meeting, and everyone got busy. Even Manny pitched in to help.

Abe called Tad aside. "Son, I want you to show Jobie what to do. He's done farm work before and he knows a lot. He just needs to learn our way of doin' it. And this is important: you must never talk about him to anyone else. Understand?"

"Yes, Sir. What about Turtle?"

"I'll talk to Turtle. Today I want you and Jobie to help yer maw get things ready and load the wagon to go down to camp meetin'."

"Sure! Thanks, Paw! C'mon Jobie! This is gonna be fun!" Jobe nodded slightly but maintained the same somber expression he had worn ever since he came in with the men.

Alice and the boys cleaned up after breakfast. In those close quarters, one thing became very apparent—Jobie needed a bath. Alice told Tad to take him down to the lake and help him to get cleaned up. "Lend 'im yer extra shirt when you come back, and I'll mend the one he has and wash it up. Now mind, don't stay down there and play. Wash and come back."

"Yes, Ma'am! C'mon Jobie!" Jobie followed with the same somber expression.

When they got down to the lake. Tad pulled off his shirt and pants and jumped in with a "Whoop!" The water still held on to the cold of winter, but the young, adventurous boy didn't pay it any attention. Jobie watched from the bank and did nothing.

"C'mon, Jobie!" Tad insisted.

Jobie just shook his head.

"What's-a matter? You scairt?"

"Ain't scairt!"

"Well git in then!"

Another defiant shake of the head.

Tad, usually the definition of patience, started out of the lake to get him. Jobie, suspicious, began to run, and a mighty chase followed. Tad was fast, but Jobie was *very* fast and it took a long time for Tad to get within reach. Not to be beat by this new-comer, Tad took a flying, head-first leap and caught Jobie around the waist. Down they both went into the new grass and dust. As they wrestled, they rolled into the mud along the lake's edge. "Maw said wash!" Tad yelled. With all his strength he pulled Jobie into the shallow water.

Jobie began to scream, "I cain't swim! I cain't swim! I gone drownd! Don't drownd me!"

"Well ya don't have to swim to wash off!" Tad screamed back. And he let go and allowed Jobie to stand up. When Jobie got his feet on the bottom and found he wouldn't sink, he finally did what Tad was showing him.

When Alice heard the door, she was stirring a pot of beans. "Well it's about time you two got back! What took you so long?" then she turned around and gazed in half-horror and half-amusement at two boys, clean . . . all the way up to their necks. Their faces and hair were still a mess of mud, grass and sweat. "What in tar-nation . . . ?"

"Maw, he was scairt to put his head in the water."

"I ain't no scairt!" Jobie screamed again and began to cry.

Alice's heart broke for the poor boy. He was obviously going to need some extra help to get accustomed to life here. "Tad, go back down to the lake and finish up."

"But, Maw . . ."

"Tad, do as yer told."

He slumped and headed back out the door.

"Tad?"

"Yes, Ma'am," he corrected himself.

"Now for you, Mr. Jobie! Did you run away from yer maw and paw and come here?"

Jobie shook his head.

Alice had heard of such things as Negro children being sold away from their mothers and fathers to work as slaves on other farms and plantations. "Did someone take you away from your mother?"

Jobie shook his head. "No, Ma'am. Sum'un took her 'way from me."

Alice's eyes teared up. She reached for the boy and hugged him close. Silently she prayed for something to say or do. Then her eyes lighted on the pies lined up by the window, cool and ready to load into the wagon. "Jobie, Darlin', do you like blueberry pie?"

"Ain't never had no blueberry pie. I heared of 'em, though."

"Would you like to try a piece?"

"Yes, Ma'am."

"All you have to do is wash yer head; then I'll give you a big piece o' blueberry pie."

Jobie was obviously wrestling with this decision.

"What if we go out back to the tub and I just pour some water over ya real gentle-like? Would you be willing to try that?"

He nodded ever so slightly, not entirely convinced. They walked back to the tub. Alice wet a rag and massaged some of her special herb soap into it. She handed the rag to Jobie and he rubbed it around on his face. Alice helped him with the back of his neck. Then she told him to close his eyes and lean over the tub and she gently poured a little water over his head. He jumped back.

"I believe I can smell that pie all the way out here," she teased.

Jobie leaned over again and allowed her to empty the bucket slowly and carefully over his head and neck. Then he immediately jumped back sputtering and shaking off like a dog.

Alice smiled approvingly. "Now you look and smell just like a fine gentleman."

Jobie smiled back a little.

"Let's go getcha some pie."

Jobie's dark, expressive eyes opened wide as Alice cut a generous slice of the thick, rich blueberry pie. He turned it around in his hands and smelled it. His mouth watered and he smiled. Then his little tongue lapped out to taste the sweet, dark berries. Such a look of ecstasy crossed his little face that it touched her heart. Then he stuck the whole thing in his mouth at once!

Suddenly, in burst Tad. "Hey! Why does he get pie?"

Before the protest was completely out of his mouth, Alice had cut another slice and handed it to Tad. Then she shrugged her shoulders. The pie was already cut and couldn't be taken to town, so she cut herself a piece, as well. All three stood chewing, some more loudly, and all three felt as though their spiritual adventure for the day had already begun. The pie was, indeed, heavenly.

Jobie could not go to the camp meeting with the rest of the family. Church or not, there were some who would be in attendance who would not appreciate the boy being there and would be suspicious whence he came. Alice dipped out a bowl of beans and collards, cut a thick slice of cornbread, and covered the rest of the cut blueberry pie. Then she led Jobie out to the barn and up into the hay loft where she deposited the food. "You'll be safe up here, Jobie. We'll be gone until tonight. If anybody comes by, just lay low. No reason anyone should venture out here." Nervous about being left alone, Jobie wrapped his arms around Alice's waist. Her eyes filled with tears. She hugged him back and impulsively kissed him on top of the head.

Stitch could not go to the camp meeting either. He also could not climb the ladder to get to the hay loft. He lay down at the bottom of the ladder, and even though Jobie was not entirely comfortable with the dog, he was glad not to be completely alone.

# A Tug on the Heart

The week continued in much the same fashion: breakfast, chores, baths, provision for Jobie, a ride down the hill, meal, camp meeting, meal, a ride home, visit with Jobie and Manny, and bed. Manny talked about a lot of things during the meetings, interesting stories of the adventures of the Israelites in Egypt, Abraham, Isaac, Jacob and Esau, David, and the Apostles. The people sat for hours and listened to Emmanuel Potter preach, but it was the private time with Manny in the evening that made the impression on Turtle.

One evening, Turtle asked Manny, "How do you do it, travellin' around all the time? I want to go places someday, maybe apprentice as a newspaper writer in Nashville, but I'd never want to leave the mountain forever. Don't you have a home? Don't you miss it?"

"Yes, Turtle. I still have a home. Haven't seen it for a while now. And, yes, it is as beautiful as Big Bear Mountain. In fact, sitting here looking down at the reflection of the stars and the moon in the lake reminds me of it very much. Yes, I love and miss my home."

"Then why do you do it?"

"Foxes have dens and birds have nests, but the Son of Man has no place to lay His head," Manny quoted. "It is the life I chose, to be a servant."

"Is that what God expects us all to do? Because I don't think I can."

"God has a plan for each one of us, Son. It's different for everyone."

"Then how can I know what to do?"

"You do just like you're doing now. You listen. He'll let you know."

And so they sat together and listened for a while, but if God was speaking to him, Turtle couldn't hear Him.

At the end of the week, Manny preached one more sermon about identity:

"My dear Friends, just the way you have been given a new name as we talked about before, it is time to allow God to form you into a new vessel for His service. He is, if you will allow me use of the word, the Potter, yes, and you are the clay. Many of us wish to go our own way, but shall the clay question the potter about what he is making? The Lord would say to you, 'Behold, as the clay is in the potter's hand, so are you in My hand.'" He continued, "'Has not the potter power over the clay to make it what he desires, a vessel for a common purpose or a vessel of honor for a special purpose?' You are clay in the hands of the great Potter who wants to prepare you either for common service: the kind that is needed consistently and dependably every day, the kind that sometimes goes unnoticed or is taken for granted and usually gets nicked or cracked along the way; or for a peculiar service: one that may be needed only once, but for a thing very great and honorable. Both different; both necessary. Will you allow God His decision for your life?"

Then, there was an opportunity for all those who had never done it to come down to Big Bear Creek to be baptized. Neither Turtle nor Tad had been baptized. After his conversations with Manny, Turtle felt it was time. Tad also expressed his desire, more because he still followed his big brother in decisions like that than because of personal conviction. Everyone walked together down the hill to Big Bear Creek and the great Emmanuel Potter walked out into the chilly, waist-deep water. From the water he recounted the story of the baptism of Jesus:

"Then cometh Jesus from Galilee to Jordon unto John, to be baptized of him. But John forbade him, saying, 'I have need to be baptized of thee, and comest thou to me?' And Jesus answering said unto him, 'Suffer it to be so now: for thus it becometh us to fulfill all righteousness.' Then he suffereth him. And Jesus, when he was baptized, went up straightway out of the water, and, lo, the heavens were opened unto him, and he saw the Spirit of God descending like a dove, and lighting upon him: And lo a voice from heaven saying, 'This is my beloved Son, in whom I am well pleased.'"

Emmanuel Potter spoke the invitation, "Would you come then, Brothers and Sisters? It also becometh you to fulfill all righteousness. Come, and be transformed."

So the people came to him as Abel and the musicians played and sang on the bank in accord with the symphonic, foaming creek. Trilliums and buttercups danced for joy in the springtime breeze while Hardy and Joe directed the people in a single-file line, and each individual who desired baptism waded out to the preacher and was lowered into the water and raised up again as Emmanuel Potter spoke the words, "Lowered in death and raised to new life. Praise the Lord!" And each time all the onlookers celebrated with shouts of praise.

When it was Turtle's turn, he boldly walked out to meet his friend, and as he was lowered into the water, all things seemed to go into slow motion, and in the rushing of the water he seemed very clearly to hear the words, "Carry my tears." Out of the water he rose and looked straight into the glistening, emerald eyes of the preacher who was smiling as he joyously exclaimed, "Praise the Lord!"

Tad followed Turtle in, but Turtle was still awed and overcome by the experience and did not see his little brother also be "lowered in death and raised up to new life." He was still pondering it when Manny came to him after the meal.

"Turtle, I want to thank you for being my friend this week. It has been an honor to get to know you and your wonderful family and to sit with you in the evenings and talk."

"You have to leave now?" Turtle had not thought this through and it troubled him.

"Yes, we're loading up the wagon right after everyone finishes eating. Thought you might like to help."

Turtle looked down and nodded his head so Manny wouldn't see the tears forming in his eyes. Manny understood, patted his shoulder and walked away.

When everything was loaded and the mules were rigged up, and Hardy was already napping in the back with his big-brimmed hat over his eyes, and Joe was sitting in the driver's seat with the reigns in his hand, Manny turned for a final farewell to the Maghee family. "Thank you for your hospitality, praise the Lord. It has been a real blessing." He shook the hands of Abel and Abe who assured him he was welcome to come back any time. Alice handed him a basket full of food for the trip to which he responded, "Thank you, Ma'am, praise the Lord. I'm sure it's delicious. We're sure gonna miss those grand meals!" He shook hands with Tad and told him, "Keep shootin' straight, Son, and look out for Jobie. He needs a friend."

Finally, Manny shook Turtle's hand, and Turtle asked, trying to be stoic, "Do you think you'll be back this way?"

"You never know," Manny replied. "We never know for sure what's around the bend. Promise me one thing, Son." Turtle nodded. "Keep listening." Turtle looked one last time into the amazing, green eyes of his friend, and something in those eyes turned his sadness into peace.

"I will, Sir."

Manny waved once more to everyone and stepped up to the bench seat in the front of the wagon beside Joe. He raised his hand as they rattled down the road and before the wagon turned the bend, they heard one final "Praise the Lord!"

Back in their own room and their own bed that night, Turtle and Tad discussed the events of the week. Turtle hesitated to speak of it, but finally asked Tad, "How did ya feel about . . . you know?"

"What?"

"About bein' baptized. How did it make ye feel?"

"It made me feel . . . all, kinda . . . clean, but inside and not outside."

"Me, too." He paused. "Did ye hear anything?

"Like what?"

"Like a voice.

"Whaddaya mean?" Tad was very sleepy.

"I heard a voice while I was under the water."

"What did it say?" He yawned.

"It said, 'Carry my tears.'"

"Carry my tears?"

"I wonder what it meant . . ."

Tad didn't answer. He was sound asleep.

# Tall Tales and True Tales

As spring passed into summer and the song of the cicadas filled the air night and day, Turtle, Tad and Jobie became very good friends. The brothers taught Jobie the workings of the Maghee farm, and Jobie jumped right in and worked side by side with the rest of the family. He began to smile more often and talk much more often, and he loved to tell stories.

One very hot, breezeless night, Turtle and Tad decided to go to the barn loft and sleep with Jobie to escape the close, stuffy air of the house. They knew the large, open hay door allowed more fresh air to enter, and the larger space allowed for circulation. That was the excuse anyway. Really they just wanted to have time to talk with Jobie about adventures and other boy stuff.

Turtle and Tad sneaked out quietly and ran as silently as they could to the dark, forbidding barn. "It sure looks differnt out here at night, Turtle," Tad remarked in a nervous whisper.

The barn door creaked eerily as they opened it and again as they closed it. They had to make their way very carefully across the floor to the ladder. Turtle went first, and Tad followed by the sound of Turtle's steps more than by sight.

"Here's the ladder," Turtle finally whispered, and he began to climb. Tad stretched out his arm in front of him until he touched a rung near the bottom, and he also started to climb. They had just reached the top and started making their way across the floor of the loft when, clink, Tad's foot bumped something. Like a shot, up jumped Jobie with a pitch fork in his hands ready to strike. In the moonlight, the brothers could see his threatening silhouette.

"Jobie! It's us!" a startled Turtle said in what was almost not a whisper as Tad jumped behind his brother for safety.

"Taaaar-nation!" Jobie responded, lowering the pitch fork. "Turtle? That you? Tad? I thought maybe you was the Skeleton of Meaty Bones come to eat my skin off."

"The what?" Turtle and Tad looked at each other.

"The Skeleton of Meaty Bones. I done met him in the woods when I was makin' my way here."

"That ain't true!" Tad barked, but he wasn't sure.

"Is true!"

"What happened then if it's so true?"

"Well si' down, and I'll tell ya."

Alice had made a nice home for Jobie up there and it was almost unfair to call his side of it a hay loft any longer. There was a cot with a down mattress and pillow, a multi-colored quilt, a brown blanket, a small rough board table with two ladder-back chairs and an oil lamp, a cup and a plate. Beside the cot was a wash stand with a white bowl and pitcher and a towel. There were hooks on the wall where Jobie could hang his few belongings. As their eyes became accustomed to the diffused moonlight in the loft, Turtle and Tad looked enviously around the little abode. They each took a seat at the table.

Jobie began: "I was walkin' in the woods. Don't know what time it was, but reckon it was aroun' midnight—the time when all the haints comes out. All of a sudden, I starts hearin' footsteps behin' me, and a kind o' rattlin'."

"Rattlin'?"

"Hush, Tad! What was it, Jobie?"

"I turns aroun', real careful-like, and there is the biggest skeleton I ever seed. Bigger than a growed man. And his teeths look like a big grin acrossed his face. And his eyes was a-glowin' with a light from inside his hade.

"'Who is you?' I asked, 'cause I'd never seed nothin' like that befo', bones a-walkin' aroun' on they own with no skin coverin' 'em.

"'I's the Skeleton of Meaty Bones, and I's gonna eat you up, so's I kin put some meat on my bones.' He says an' he laughs a terrible laugh.

"'Oh, no, you ain't says I,' and I takes off runnin'.

"So the Skeleton of Meaty Bones call for his brothers, Starkin and Hairkin, and they all begin to chase me through them woods. Purty soon, Starkin was right behin' me, but I ducks under a low hangin' branch, and Starkin' runs slap dab into it and knocks 'is hade clean off 'is neck and falls down dade!"

Turtle and Tad laughed at that.

50

"'Then here come Hairkin right behin' me, so I runs to a big rock hangin' over a loooooong drop. It was so far down and I almos' fell down it myself, but I move out the way jus' in time, and Hairkin went a-fallin' over the edge and 'is bones busted all apart down below."

The boys laughed again.

"So then it was jus' me and the Skeleton of Meaty Bones, and he come a-chasin' me through them woods a-shoutin' . . ."

Jobie didn't have time to finish, because at that moment a booming voice came from the direction of the ladder saying, "I come to eat all of ye up and put meat on my bones!"

The three boys jumped up and ran to the back of the loft trying desperately to find a place to hide! Stitch began to bark hysterically from the floor below! All of a sudden, the story seemed to have become true!

Then came laughter, and it was laughter they all recognized. A light appeared in a lantern, and there was Abel, standing in his long johns and hat with tears pouring down his face from uncontrollable amusement. "Y'all's faces!" He just kept repeating, "Y'all's faces!"

"Grampaw!" The boys yelled.

"How'd you know we were here?" Turtle asked.

"Y'all didn't think ye could sneak out the house without somebody hearin' ye, did ye?"

"You heard us?" Tad was amazed. Both boys had thought their grandfather was becoming a bit hard-of-hearing.

"Weeeeeeeellllll, no, it weren't exactly me heard ye," Abel admitted. "It was yer maw, and she come and woke me up and told me to foller ye."

That sounded more credible. They could never hide anything from their maw.

"Was she mad, Grampaw?" Tad was feeling guilty.

"Naw. She just didn't know where y'all were headed and she didn't want anybody to git hurt." He sat down on the hay and tossed a bag of nuts out in front of him. The boys scrambled to get some, amazed at this unexpected treat. They all sat down with their grandfather around the lamp and chomped. "It is nice and cool up here, ain't it?"

The boys nodded.

"You tell us a story, Grampaw," Turtle said.

"A story? Let me see . . . a story . . . 'bout twenty year ago I was a-fishin' down at the narrow end of the lake. All of a sudden, the biggest black bear I done ever seen walks down to the bank acrossed from me. We was only about thirty yards from each other, so I seen 'im good, and I seen what happened real good, too.

"Well, that bear come into the water and commenced a-fishin'. Fish after fish he caught on his claws and slung 'em up on the bank 'til he had ten big fish. Guess he figured that was enough 'cause he come up out the water a-lickin' his chops and ready to eat.

"Suddenly, out of the woods come this huge critter, all furry and 'bout ten feet tall. It had ten arms a-wavin' in the air and a little, tiny head with some big ol' teeth in it. It was a-hissin' and a-screechin' to high heaven. Well that bear, he stood lookin' in shock for a minute, then takes off into the woods leavin' all his fish behind." The boys laughed at that.

Abel continued, "As soon as the bear was gone, the critter got quiet, and then . . . it begin to come apart! Dadgum if it weren't five raccoons stacked up on each other's shoulders, tails wrapped around 'em hidin' their faces, 'cept for the one on top. Each one of them raccoons run and grabbed one fish in its mouth and another fish in its hands, and off they run on two feet like little people.

"Yep, that poor bear went hungry that day, but the raccoons et purdy good." The boys were literally rolling on the floor laughing by the end of the tale.

"Time to sleep now, boys," Abel announced. "The sun'll be up early and we need to be up with it." He lay back in the hay, and before long he was snoring.

"Jobie?" Tad whispered.

"Yeah." Jobie answered.

"Are you still awake?"

"Yeah."

"Tell me what it was like where you lived before."

"Don't like to think 'bout it much, Tad."

"I figerred it must be purdy bad."

"Wors'en bad, 'though it weren't always that way. When I were real little, I lived with my mama and pap just like you do, and I had six brothas and two sistas. I was the youngest. We lived on Colonel Fraley's land. I don't know as I eva met

Colonel Fraley, but he were always bein' talked about. Folks say he had a gamblin' problem an' was 'dicted to opium.

"One day two men come an' take my oldest brotha away. I jus' rememba him a little. Befo' he lef' he lean ova an' look me in the eyes an' tell me, 'Jobie, work hard. It always he'p when ya works hard.' Then they takes 'im away and I neva sees 'im agin. The nex' one they come fo' was my pap. He tried to fight 'em, but it weren't no good. They put 'im in chains. Even in them chains, he hug me real hard befo' he go, an' tell me he love me. Tears was in his eyes. I never see my pap cry befo' that, not even when they beat 'im bloody 'cause they say he took somthin' didn't belong to 'im, but he didn't take it. He always taught us stay outta trouble.

"Seem like it happen with fo' mo' brothas, jus' the same, an' one sista. Then one day they come fo' my last brotha, William. He say to me, 'Jobie, they sellin' us to pay off Colonel Fraley gamblin' debts. We ain't neva goin' see each otha agin. You look afta Mama and Mary (Mary was my baby sista), and when you kin git away, take off an' run fo' ye life. Run no'th far as ye kin, an' take 'em with ye as far as ye kin.' Then he was gone, too.

"They leave us alone fo' a while afta that, I don't know how long. Then one day I seed Granny Silvy talkin' to Mama and Mama looked scairt. That night she wake me up an' tell me we leavin' and be real quiet. We took off out behind the house and kep on goin' all night. When daylight come, we hid in the woods. We keep on like that fo' days. That when Mary start to git sick. Mama did all she knowed to do to he'p her. She even sing to her real quiet. But Mary kep' on cryin', and then a group of men find us. Mama say to me, 'Run, boy,' so I run, and then I heared a shot behind me. I look around and my mama was layin' on the ground on top o' Mary, and she was bleedin' and the cryin' was stopped.

"I hid 'til the men went by; then I went back to Mama. She was dade. Mary weren't dade, but she weren't cryin' no more either, and she look kinda funny. I pick up Mary and sit beside Mama, an' then I fell asleep. When I wake up, a man standin' there—a man with green eyes, real green like Preacha Manny's—an' he tell me he goin' take me to a place where it safe. He look at Mary and touch her real gentle, and she smile and fall asleep. Then he say somethin' strange. He say, *Carry my tears*. So I picks up Mary and follows that man. We walk a long way, and then we come to a ol' church, and they's singin' comin' out that church. We walks in an' I's awful tired. A man and woman comes up to me, and I hands Mary to 'em an' I says, 'Her name Mary.' They take her an' I walk out. Then I follow the man here. I never seen him agin' since the day yo' paw brought me in."

Tad was sitting up now, slowly shaking his head and not knowing how to respond.

"What did you say that man said to you?" Turtle asked. The other two jumped a little. They hadn't realized that Turtle was listening.

"The man in the woods with the green eyes, what did you say he told you?"

"He say, 'Carry my tears.' I don't rightly know what he meant, 'cep' to git Mary to a safe place," Jobie replied.

"Carry my tears," Tad repeated and looked at Turtle.

Tad could see Turtle's eyes shining in the wane light from the hay door, but he did not answer.

# Blood Brothers

As the fall fair approached, Tad and Jobie spent much of their free time hunting. Tad prided himself on bringing in the "big buck" award nearly every year with his old but trusty Hawken rifle, a faithful friend that had gone to the woods and fields with him many times and bought his family countless pounds of meat and useful skins. In addition, for his accomplishments he had won a gold coin, a fine leather coat, and a pair of boots, as well as chickens and once, a bull. This year, the prize made Tad's mouth water and his heart beat fast. It was a brand new twin trigger .44 caliber Rimfire Wesson. The rifle hung on display in the Big Bear General Store, and Tad believed it was the most beautiful thing he had ever seen. He only had to bag that big buck one more time.

Jobie had never hunted before he came to live with the Maghees, and all he knew about it, he had learned from Tad. He was a quick learner though, and a very intuitive hunter. Jobie had learned to use Abel's daddy's old Revolutionary War rifle, and with it had brought in ducks, turkeys, and two small deer. Often Jobie and Tad would take off for the woods early in the morning while the moon gilded the hilltops and the clouds swathed the valleys, and they wouldn't return until late afternoon. Once they got into trouble for setting out on such a morning and not returning until much after dark that night, determined that they would not come in until both had something to show for their hunt. Abe, Abel and Turtle had gone out in search of them, afraid they had fallen upon some accident making them unable to return home and met them on the path by the barn. From there, they had to endure Abe's cold stare, Abel's fiery lecture, and probably the worst of all, Alice's tears.

Tad and Jobie were on such a hunt one morning while the frost nipped the corn stalks and the moon looked like light was being squeezed from it, when the biggest buck Tad had ever seen passed majestically in front of them.

"Eight point, Tad! Did you see?" Jobie's whisper was only heard because he was almost standing on top of Tad. "An' they spread nearly as wide as the barn doors!"

Tad couldn't answer. Even allowing for distortion caused by shadows, it was the biggest buck he had ever seen.

Carefully . . . quietly . . . stealthily . . . the boys began to track it. Dawn was beginning to break. Soon it would be easier to see. A movement. The boys moved a little apart. Another movement. The buck was close. They shouldered their rifles . . . annnnnnd . . . crash! Like a bolt between the trees, the buck lunged toward them. So taken by surprise at the aggression of this animal, Tad's rifle was knocked from his grasp and the razor sharp hooves of the deer sliced his right arm and leg. Tad buckled in shock and pain as the deer turned on Jobie who tried to fire, but in an effort not to hit Tad, aimed too high. The buck was not frightened and still had his eyes on Tad. Jobie was not willing to let his friend be torn to shreds by this maniacal animal and jumped between them, rifle ready, but before he could get off a shot, he was also struck down, rifle knocked ten feet away, and hooves, like daggers, cutting into his left leg and foot. The king of deer then stood before his kneeling, bleeding victims, snorted loudly, and pranced off, unharmed, into the woods, not looking back.

For a moment, there was only the sound of loud breathing. Finally, Jobie spoke:

"You alive, Tad?"

"I'm hurt pretty bad, Jobie. You?"

"I'm bleedin'. I thinks he tried to cut off ma foot."

"Can you walk?"

"I don't know. We have to git home somehow."

The boys dragged themselves closer together, then helped each other to stand. Putting their injured sides together and holding each other up, they began the slow trek home. Stitch, sensing a problem, left his favorite chore of helping Turtle with the milking, his job, to taste the product, and ran off into the woods. He found the boys at nearly the end of their strength. Never had they felt so relieved!

"Stitch, go git Turtle," Tad ordered.

Stitch barked and hesitated.

"Git, Turtle! Go!"

Stitch turned and made his way back to the farm as fast as he could go.

He got Abel's attention first, "Tar-nation! What's wrong with that dog?"

"What is it, Stitch. C'm'er, boy!" Turtle ordered.

Stitch turned back toward the woods barking. Then again toward Turtle and Abel.

"Something's wrong. He wants us to follow him. Paw!"

Abe came around the corner of the barn, and all three men took off behind the insistent dog. He led them straight to Tad and Jobie, who were still struggling to hold each other up and limping slowly forward. What a frightening sight they were, bloodied and dirty, inching down a path that was now light enough to reveal their injuries. The three men rushed to them and half carried them the rest of the way back. Stitch ran ahead to alert Alice.

When the group came into sight, Alice's heart skipped a beat. There was so much blood! They laid the boys out in the kitchen and began to clean the wounds. Alice prayed out loud as she prepared to stitch up the gaping wounds left by the sharp hooves of the mighty deer. Abel came in with his Christmas whiskey and gave the boys each a stout drink straight from the bottle. Then Abel and Abe held the boys down as Alice stitched. Herb compresses were applied and the boys were wrapped up warm and made as comfortable as possible. After another swig of the whiskey, they fell into a restless sleep.

After everything was cleaned up and the house was put back to right, Turtle walked quietly into the room where the two injured boys had been placed on the bed. He hugged his mother who was keeping watch and wiping the sweat off their foreheads every few minutes. He petted Stitch, the hero of the day, who kept vigil over the two boys. Then he walked over to Tad, placed a hand on his head, and whispered a quiet prayer. He did the same for Jobie.

"My little preacher-man," Alice said softly.

"I'm not a preacher-man," he answered and left the room.

Tad woke in the night. It was dark and he was in his bed and his body seemed to hurt everywhere. Alice, still close by, heard him groan. She came over to the bed and swabbed his feverish forehead with a cold, wet cloth.

"We was so scairt for ye, Son. When y'all came through that door, all I could see was blood, both of ye covered in it. We couldn't tell if it was yer blood on Jobie or Jobie's blood on you. Turned out, it was both."

"We blood brothers, then." Jobie was awake, but his voice was very husky. "They says if one man's blood get mixed with another man's blood, from that day they blood brothers."

"Blood brothers," Tad answered. "I reckon so."

Tad missed the "big buck" that year and didn't win the rifle; however, in his heart he felt he had won something infinitely more valuable.

# Rumors of Wars

Seasons came and went in Big Bear, and for the most part, the world left the tiny, peaceful spot alone; however, in the early spring of 1860, when Turtle was 17, Tad was 15, and Jobie was called 15 as well, because, of course, no one really knew, Alice's brother Paul came up the mountain. Abe caught sight of him from the cornfield where they were just beginning to break ground for the season. "Tad," he called, "go tell yer Maw we got comp'ny." Tad took off like a hound after a rabbit, and when Alice heard the news, she went into a tizzy of spontaneous preparation. By the time the gentlemen arrived at the door, the table was heavy with dried fruit, biscuits, butter, cheese and sliced ham—a feast for a travelling relative and a welcome mid-day treat for the Maghee men.

At first the conversation revolved around family and memories and there was laughter, but soon there was a turn to more serious topics.

"You know," said Paul, "that I have always been a loyal supporter of our United States and I'm not about to turn my back now, but trouble's brewin', and before long we may all need to make some decisions we don't much care for. In South

Carolina there's talk of secession, and I hear tell that in Georgia and Alabama the locals are takin' over the military, formin' their own militias, seizin' control of the forts. The South is preparin' to defend herself."

"Paul," Abel argued, "they're just over-reactin' to rumors."

"They're more than rumors, Sir. And if you value the life y'all have on this mountain, you'd better be ready to defend it, 'cause when those Yanks get control, our lives are gonna change. Tennessee is the breadbasket of the whole nation. How do you think they plan to feed those soldiers?"

"We got rifles, and we can shoot," Tad piped in. "Ain't no Yanks gonna take anything from us."

"You boys go on now," Alice said, shooing Tad and Jobie out the door. "Paul, don't you go an' get the boys all worked up. Ain't nothing happened yet they should be a-worryin' about."

Tad and Jobie left the room, but they did not go far. They wanted to hear what was said.

"Abel, Abe," Paul demanded quietly, glancing toward the door on the other side of which the boys were hidden, "I want to know just what has taken over your minds."

"Not sure what yer askin', Paul," Abel's voice was tense.

"Don't you know what kind of trouble you can get into up here hidin' that darkie?"

"We don't use that word here, Paul," Abe returned.

Abel asked, "What makes ye think we're hidin' anyone?"

Paul viciously pointed his finger, though his voice remained quiet. "You know what I'm a-talkin' about."

"People have seen Jobie workin' for us. He's a free Negro; nobody 'round here seems to mind a bit," Turtle said, feeling privileged to have been allowed to stay with the grown-ups. "He works just as hard as we do!"

"No matter what you call it, it don't change the facts. Them darkies ain't like us and treatin' 'im like he is will only bring ye trouble."

"That's enough!" Abe stood up and slammed his fists on the table. His chair hit the floor behind him. "This is our home and yer welcome in it, but if ye don't like what goes on here, yer also welcome to leave!" He walked out so quickly that he didn't even notice the boys hiding on the other side of the door. Turtle followed him out.

"Paul," Alice began, although she usually did not participate in the conversations of the men, "you know you been raised to have more compassion than that."

Paul hissed, "*You* know that husband o' yourn is endangerin' you and the boys by harborin' a run-a-way slave."

Abel came around the corner and shooed Tad and Jobie down toward the lake as Alice declared, "I stand by ma husband, Paul."

"What he mean I'm a-dangerin' y'all, Mr. Abel? I ain't done nothin' to nobody."

"No, Jobie," Abel tried to be comforting, "but folks kin be mighty confused and git all in a tizzy over't. There's them that wouldn't cotton to ye bein' here with us and not bein' a slave, but it's 'cause they don't know ye like we do. Let's git back to work."

When the men came in that evening, Paul was gone. Alice didn't say much during dinner, nor afterward as they sat together and Turtle read from the Bible as he always did, but as the boys headed to bed that night, she hugged Jobie just a little longer than usual, and whispered, "Always know yer loved, Jobie. You got a family. Always know that."

* * *

Manny did not return for camp meeting that summer. The evangelist, a Reverend Moody, was a powerful man of God. Abel and the other musicians played and sang, the grannies danced and marched, and many were saved, healed, and filled with the Holy Ghost during his visit. However, Turtle's mind was somewhere else. Not that he had abandoned his faith, but he found a new object of his petitions to the Master. Her name was Callalily Norton.

Callalily lived at the foot of Big Bear Mountain in a lovely home with her maw, paw (who was the town apothecary), and four sisters, who were all named after flowers. She was not new to Big Bear and Turtle's family had known her family quite well for years. The odd thing was that Turtle had barely noticed her before. She was like a mountain laurel whose leafy branches you might pass by for a year not noticing, until one spring day, out of that ordinary green there arises a profusion of snowy white blossoms that stop you in your tracks for their stunning beauty and fragrance. That's what it was like to Turtle when he lifted his eyes from the task of unloading the wagon one afternoon just as Callalily walked onto the camp meeting grounds. She was dressed in white and barefoot, carrying a basket of fresh-baked bread, her auburn hair glistening in the sun. She was surrounded by her sisters and some friends but Turtle saw no one but her.

Alice took notice and said, "Y'all hurry and get this food unloaded. Maybe those Norton's could use some help."

Turtle needed no further encouragement and strode directly up to Callalily, offering to carry her basket for her. Callalily stopped in her tracks and shyly nodded, eyes to the ground. The other girls giggled and walked around them.

As Turtle reached to take the basket of bread, his hand brushed against Callalily's hand and a thrill jolted his heart. Without saying a word, he walked beside her to a table and set down the basket, then followed her into the meeting house. He sat beside her, and that was all he knew about the service that day. They did not speak or even look at each other. For the moment, just being next to her was enough.

When the assembly was dismissed and everyone went out to the grounds to eat, Callalily turned and waved to Turtle as she rejoined her family. He was disappointed because he would like to have stayed with her through the meal, and this abrupt dismissal confused him. Maybe he should have said something to her. Yes, that would have made a difference. Tomorrow . . . tomorrow would be different. Turtle went off to join his family and friends, as well.

The talk of the men as they gathered together in groups was all about trouble brewing:

"Been near 'bout six months since the fiasco at Harper's Ferry. Did y'all see it in the papers? Ol' John Brown and his men took control of the federal buildins and then took hostages. One of 'em was a relative of George Washington, hisself. Then when the shootin' began, the first one to git shot was a free Negro, jus' because he didn't answer 'em right," said one middle-aged man that Turtle had seen often at the General Store.

Big Bear General Store owner Charles Compton went on, "A lot of people was kilt because of John Brown's doin's. He paid for it, too—hanged by the neck for treason he was!"

"Maybe what he did weren't right," added Timmy Crowder, a young man who had attended school with Turtle several years back but had to quit to help out in his family's saw mill, "but he had right reasons."

"And what right reasons was that, young'un?" It was the middle-aged man again.

"He meant to do away with the abomination of slavery," returned Timmy.

"They's some that don't call it an abomination, Boy," said the middle-aged man. "They's some that would say the abomination is makin' those Negroes equal to you an' me."

"Well, I admire what the man was tryin' to do, though I cain't agree with his methods." That was Abe.

"'Course you do, Abe Maghee," Compton replied. "You got one a-livin' up there with you! And he ain't no slave. Y'all treat him like kin. Look! He's a-sittin' over there with yer people right now." It was true that since everyone around Big

Bear had seen Jobie working on the farm or at least heard about him, the Maghees had become less concerned about him joining them for social events as long as he stayed with the family.

"Yer right, he ain't no slave. I don't own slaves, and neither do you, ner anyone else in these parts, Charles Compton," Abe replied.

"All I'm sayin' is you best be careful. They's talk of secession in South Carolina right now. Once states start takin' sides, things for people like y'all are gonna git dangerous right quickly."

Abe left the group, and Turtle followed him. The men continued to murmur about the issue, but the Maghees had had their fill.

# Love

That night, Turtle's thoughts were not about slaves, nor about secession; his thoughts were about Callalily Norton. He went over and over their next meeting, rehearsing in his mind what he would do and say. Tad and Jobie found it very odd that he should be so quiet.

Finally Tad asked, "What's eatin' away at you, Turtle?"

Turtle smiled and sighed a long sigh, thinking if he didn't answer, maybe the boys would think he was asleep. No luck.

Jobie tossed a pillow at him and demanded, "Turtle! What wrong with you?"

"Okay, y'all wanna know? I'm in love. I'm gonna marry Callalily Norton." It felt good to say it.

For a moment there was silence. Then hysterical laughter from the two younger boys.

"Haaaahaaaahaaaaa! He say he goin' git marrit . . ."

"To Callalily!!! Haaahaaaaahaaaaaaaaa . . ."

Turtle could not be shaken now that the words had come out of his mouth. He liked the way they sounded, and he liked the way he felt when he said them. Tossing the pillow back at

Jobie, he chuckled quietly. "Y'all just a couple o' babies, that's all."

The younger boys continued to laugh, but Stitch came over and licked Turtle's hand. Turtle petted him on his flat, fuzzy head and resumed his daydream.

The next morning, everyone was up bright and early to finish chores before it was time to leave for camp meeting. When Turtle had completed his part, he ran up to the house to get one of Alice's cakes of soap. Then he ran down to the lake and jumped in. The water was fiercely cold, but he wanted desperately to be at his best that day. After the bath, he returned to his room to dress in his "meetin' clothes." They were not freshly washed, as he had worn his black pants and white shirt the day before to the church, but they were his best. In addition, he borrowed a slim black tie from Abel, who showed him how to tie it crossed over in front and pin it up with a shiny gold pin, his only possession of elegance in the world, not because he could not have afforded a few nice things, but because he simply wasn't interested. The tie was a gift from his dear Nancy when they were both young and very much in love. Abel wasn't one to ask questions. He had seen his grandson sitting beside the lovely auburn-haired girl in the meeting and he knew how to add things up.

"Be careful with it Turtle; or maybe it's time to start calling you Caleb agin, ye reckon?" he asked as he straightened the boy's collar. "Shucks, just keep it. It's meant to come to you, anyway." He patted the young man on the back and sent him on his way.

Turtle was impatient to leave for the meeting, but there was nothing he could do but wait until the others were ready. Eventually, though, everyone piled into the wagon along with another day's worth of food offerings, and they were off. When the food was unloaded onto the appropriate table, Turtle began to watch the horizon for the Nortons. For a long time he didn't see any of them and he began to worry; however, Alice was watching her son, and she was also watching the Norton girls who had arrived before them. She gently touched her elder son on the shoulder and pointed toward the middle of the laughing, happy crowd of boys and girls. There she was, lovelier than the image he had kept in his mind. Auburn curls bounced on her shoulders as she walked and sparkling blue eyes lit up her freckled face.

Turtle walked over to her quickly before he could lose his nerve and cleared his throat to get her attention. "Miss Norton, may I escort you to the meetin' house?" He used his best, educated speaking style and offered her his arm.

Some of the others around her giggled, while some stared with wide eyes as she answered, "Why, thank you, Mr. Maghee," and laced her arm in his. Turtle glowed. She knew his name!

They walked off to the door of the church and entered arm-in-arm. They found a place to sit on one of the benches with the adults. Turtle got very caught up in the worship, clapping his hands and singing along as Abel and his group seemed to call down heaven with their music, and the grannies danced like they were on streets of gold. Afterward though, as the preaching began, Turtle was very aware of the girl next to him. He looked over at her hands clasped in her lap. They were small and seemed very clean. He looked down at his own hands, a little bit ashamed of the farm stains around his fingernails. Callalily must have noticed because she gracefully placed one hand on the bench between them. His heart pounded but he did not move. Then she looked up at him through her long lashes. Her blue eyes met his and she smiled just a little, then looked back toward the preacher. He very slowly moved his hand until it touched hers. She didn't flinch or pull away. He cautiously curled his fingers around hers.

*Thwack!*

The fan belonging to Mrs. Clara Jemison who was sitting directly behind them, came down on top of his hand!

"Hey! . . . uhhh . . . men! Amen!" he cried and jerked his hand back into his lap as Callalily giggled a tiny giggle.

Several men around them who had begun to doze off were roused by his outburst and also exclaimed, "Amen!"

Reverend Moody, inspired by the response, preached on with renewed vigor.

As Turtle walked Callalily home that evening, just behind her group of sisters and just ahead of her parents, she asked him, "Why did your parents give you such a strange name, Turtle?"

"My parents?" he was confused. Oh, you mean, *Turtle.* That's not my real name. I mean, that's what everybody has called me ever since I was seven, but my given name is *Caleb.*" He went on to tell her the story of his encounter with the snapping turtle, laughing at the end as most people did when they heard the story for the first time.

Her response, however, was, "Caleb . . . Mr. Caleb Maghee . . . yes, I like that name. It's much more grown-up than *Turtle*."

That night, Turtle announced to his family that he no longer wished to be referred to as *Turtle*, but would henceforth answer to his given name, *Caleb*.

After that, Caleb spent more and more of his free time with Callalily and her family. Tad was hurt and confused about his brother's aloof behavior and sudden desertion, but Caleb assured him that he would understand someday and that they would always be brothers no matter what happened.

The highland meadows filled with deer and yellow butterflies. Rhododendrons burst into pink and lavender blossoms. Cotton clouds tipped with pink and gold skimmed across the wide, blue sky. The lake seemed to be studded with jewels, whether under the sun or the moon, and the creek sang mysterious love songs as it frolicked over smooth rocks on its way to the Tennessee. It seemed an enchanted summer for Caleb and Callalily.

Even without his brother, Tad never had to face an adventure on his own. Jobie and Stitch enjoyed hunting and fishing as much as he did, and Abel, who seemed to be living out his second childhood, was also a fine companion.

They had much to distract them, but the boys began to notice that Alice was acting strangely. She still completed all her daily chores as she always had, and she still baked her special pies, but she had taken to being ill rather often and required extended time to rest. She moved a chair to the kitchen and did much of her cooking preparation sitting down. Then one evening, shortly after Caleb returned from visiting at the Norton's house, Abe called the family together.

"Paw, boys, we got somethin' to tell ye. Seems the good Lord don't think our family is complete yet. We're gonna have another young'un, 'pears 'round February. Boys, yer maw wants to keep this private fo' while, hear?" It was Abe's way not to say a lot, and that was that. Announcement made. The rest of the family, full of questions but in too much shock to ask them, took their turns hugging Alice and kissing her on the cheek very gently, almost as if this new development made them afraid she might break.

# Decision

Just as the Maghee family was changing during this time, the state of the country was changing, as well. Remote as it was, Big Bear was being drawn into the turmoil of North verses South. One day in early autumn, as the leaves were just beginning to turn gold and the pumpkins were ripening to orange, the men of the community were called to the meeting house for an important speech. It was such an unusual occurrence that everyone believed it must be a matter of life and death, and to some, indeed, it would become just that.

The Maghee males and Jobie arrived together. Men in uniform and men in suits were standing outside the door, making the simple, rustic building look quite important.

"Sir, I don't think ye want to be bringin' yer slave inside."

"He's not a slave."

"I don't think ye want to be bringin' *him* (he indicated Jobie) inside."

"Tad, Jobie, go wait for us at home," Abe answered.

"But Paw!"

"Home, Tad."

"Yes, Sir."

The boys walked off with their heads hung low, and Abe, Abel and Caleb went inside. The meeting house was full and stuffy, and smelled of sweat. They found a place to stand along the wall with others who had just arrived. Shafts of sunlight entered in through narrow windows and lit the dust motes that hovered on the currents of breath. No one said much. The atmosphere was thick with tension.

Finally, Brother Edwards approached the lectern with a gray-haired, heavy-set man in a dark suit:

"Brothers of Big Bear, Angel Head, Finnysville, and Franklin: As you know, our country is about to take part in a very important Presidential election. You have been called here today to hear the words of a gentleman from Chattanooga, Mr. Harold Lowery, who has important information regarding that election. Give him now your undivided attention.

The gray-haired, heavy-set man stepped forward and took Brother Edward's place at the lectern. "Gentlemen: Thank you for coming. I am Harold Lowery, known to some of you as the attorney for the people from Hamilton County. I am here to speak to you today about a very important issue that concerns all of us who love this great state of Tennessee, and who do not want it to fall to the tyranny of a group of men in Washington who desire to place us under the rule of a despotic monarch." There were some cheers from the crowd.

"The question, my friends, is this: Was the Republic of which we are a part intended to be a unified nation in which all individual states resign their sovereign rights and identities forever, or is it a federation of sovereign states which joined together for a specific purpose, namely, freedom from the tyranny of England, and from which they can withdraw at any time?"

Cries of "We won't give up our freedom!" and "We don't need Washington!" erupted from the crowd.

Lowery continued, "Shall we exchange one dictator for another?"

"Noooooooooo!" returned the crowd.

"Then let me speak to you of the presidential election which is close upon us. Four men stand ready to take that most important office. There is Stephen Douglas, a Democrat, a Southern gentleman and a slave-owner, who should believe in the preservation of the life we Southerners, are living. Yet, he acts as a traitor, favoring popular sovereignty and standing with the Union no matter the cost to us, even if it is to compromise our way of life and belief.

Next, there is John Breckenridge, Kentucky-born, a Democrat. He demands federal intervention to protect the Southern plantations and farms to protect slave-owners on one side, but insists he is not anti-Union on the other. He says he believes that slavery cannot be banned in a territory that is not yet a state, yet he leaves the decisions for the states themselves up to the federal government. Now I ask you once again, do you want men who are miles away from here in Washington to tell you what is best for Tennessee?"

The answer was a reverberating, "Noooooooooooo!"

Lowery continued, "From Illinois, there is the Republican Abraham Lincoln, a lawyer who would say to us, and I quote, 'A house divided against itself cannot endure, permanently half slave and half free. I do not expect the Union to be dissolved. I do not expect the house to fall. But I do expect it will cease to be divided,' and friends, his sympathies are with the North, the very ones who would destroy our beloved Southern way of life!"

There was a chorus of "Boooooooo!"

"Then, my friends, there is a great man of Tennessee who stands ready to serve us in Washington. He has already tirelessly served seven, yes friends, seven terms in Congress. He was the secretary of War under William Henry Harrison. He has lived afar, but has kept his beloved Tennessee close in his mind and heart. That faithful man, friends, is Mr. John Bell!" Mr. Lowery pulled a brass bell from his pocket and began to ring it loudly as the crowd cheered. "John Bell is a man acquainted with the ways of Washington and well-prepared to lead this country, both North and South. When he has been elected to the office of President of the United States of America, Tennessee will no longer fear the tyrant federal government. Our state legislature will be able to make decisions based on what is best for Tennessee. No man's property, for which he has justly paid, will be taken away from him. No man will be denied the ability to run his farm or plantation because his slaves have been taken away. We will all sleep well at night, assured that our children will know the same freedoms that we have known. (There was a tumult of cheers.) God bless you! God bless John Bell! And God bless Tennessee! (Cheers shook the building.) Let freedom ring!"

Lowery rang his bell again and several men passed bells out to the crowd. Soon, the air was splitting with the ringing of bells and chants of the name of John Bell, a man who none of the folk of Big Bear had ever met.

Mr. Lowery walked through the middle of the group shaking hands. He mounted his waiting horse outside the meeting house and waved his hat in farewell to the group of men who had followed him outside. His entourage mounted horses as well, and all of them raced off down the road toward the next small town.

As the mounted politicians disappeared from sight and the chaos diminished, the men of Big Bear discussed what they had heard. Most of them seemed to agree that a Tennessee man would have their interests more at heart than anyone else. The large group broke into smaller groups, then into twos and threes headed back to work for the afternoon, feeling quite secure in their choice.

Abel, Abe and Caleb walked without speaking for a while. It was getting harder for Abel to climb the mountain, but he was too stubborn to ride the mule. Abe and Caleb slowed their steps some to stay beside the old man. Abel was the first one to break the silence.

"What do y'all think about that then?"

"Reckon it might be good to have a Tennessee man," Abe replied noncommittally.

"Reckon so," Abel replied.

And that was that.

*Sometimes being a man*, Caleb thought, *is a very confusing thing.*

* * *

The fair came that fall with the usual excitement and the unusual buzz of election propaganda which almost overshadowed the other activities. Prize hogs and bulls were named for the candidates, ribbons were passed out along with voting directions, and a red, white and blue pie contest was held. Quilts with the colors of America, alongside black bears, flowers, butterflies and geometric patterns were on display to sell.

Tad won the big buck contest and got another gold coin, and Alice, who could not be held back by pregnancy, won the pie contest with blueberries, strawberries and fresh cream on the flakiest crust this side of heaven.

Caleb was asked to read from the United States Declaration of Independence on the final night. As he read, a fight broke out. It was quickly brought under control, but it was painfully obvious that the raw nerves of the rest of the country had made their way into Big Bear. Many thought it fortunate that the election would be over soon and things could return to normal, but others feared that no matter what the outcome of the election, things would never be the same again.

Then came the fateful date of November 6. Ballots were cast. Everyone waited. At dawn on November 8, copies of *The*

*Tennessee Patriot* finally arrived at the Big Bear general store. Shots rang out from those men who had been appointed to wait for the news, and the community moved in like a tidal wave to hear that although not a single Tennessee ballot had been cast in his favor, Abraham Lincoln was the new President of the United States of America.

# Callalily

It was an unusually pleasant morning a couple weeks after the election when Caleb asked to speak privately with his mother. After breakfast was cleared away, he remained in the kitchen with Alice, who was blossoming at the end of her second trimester. She smiled gently as she linked her arm into that of her elder son and led him into the keeping room.

"Put a log or two on that fire, Darlin', and come sit by me. It's been a long time since it was just you and me here to talk."

"Yes, Ma'am."

"When you were just a baby I used to rock you in this very chair. You had the sweetest eyes, and you'd look right up at me like you could still remember all the mysteries ever'body else done forgot. You still look that way sometimes, my little preacher-man."

"Maw, I know you've always said that, but I just don't feel inclined to be a preacher-man. I think God has to call you to do that, or somethin'. I can't live the kind of life a preacher-man has to live."

"What kind of life is that, Son?

"Well, remember how Manny travelled all over the place and didn't see his home in years? It was the same with all those preachers at camp meetin'."

"Your grampaw is a preacher. He has a home. So does Brother Edwards and Brother Hugh. Brother Nettles has a house in Kady's Pass."

"Yes, Ma'am, but Brother Nettles, well, his wife died a long time ago—I don't even remember her—and Brother Edwards' wife took their kids and done run off from him, and after all, he and Brother Hugh and Grampaw are only part-time preachers. Remember Manny? He has Hardy and Joe, but they never go home, no wives or families."

"Is that what you want to talk about, Son?" Caleb dropped his head and nodded. "Ohhhhhh, I thought I done seen that look in yer eye. Callalily Norton?"

"Yes, Ma'am."

"You know y'all still mighty young."

"Yes, Ma'am, but not much younger than you and Paw were when you got married. And, well, even if I ask her, we couldn't get married for a while. I need to be makin' a good livin' first."

"Always been a good livin' to be made right here. Corn's not goin' out of style."

"Not gonna be a farmer, Maw. I want to be a writer, maybe for some big-city newspaper in Nashville or Memphis.

"Caleb! Would ye leave the mountain, Son?" Alice's eyes searched his. She always knew the day would come when her little birds would leave the nest, but she didn't expect it would be so soon. "I s'pose you'd like to see the ring, then," she added with a note of melancholy.

"Yes, Ma'am."

Alice had worn only her plain gold wedding band for years. Hard work threatened the pale blue aquamarine stone in the delicate silver filigree setting that had belonged to Abel's wife Nancy, and that Abe had given her on the day they were pledged to marry. Now she walked over to the loose boards behind the stairs and bent to retrieve a small velvet box. Afraid she would fall, Caleb rushed over to help her up and replace the boards. Alice smiled at her son as she opened the box and took out the lovely ring, holding it up so the light from the fire shone through the translucent stone.

"It's mighty pretty, isn't it, Maw?"

"You sure, Son? You sure she's the one?"

"Yes, Ma'am."

"Does yer paw know?"

"Not yet, but Grampaw does. He told me to ask you for it."

Alice took her son's hand then, and with one of her small, strong hands she held it, palm up. With the other hand she placed the precious ring into that palm and closed his fingers over it. They looked into each other's nearly identical coffee-brown eyes and smiled. Alice patted his hands one more time. "Your hands done got so big. You're not a baby any more, but those eyes still hold all the mysteries of the world. God bless you, Caleb. Y'all be happy, hear?"

"Yes, Ma'am." Caleb hugged Alice close. It had been a long time since he had thought about how much he loved her, and now with the realization that he would not much longer see her face at breakfast or hear her singing in the garden, his heart felt like it would burst. Until that moment, Caleb had only thought of where he was going, not what he was leaving behind.

Alice broke the spell. "Go on with ye then," she said in the tone she used when it was time to go to school. "Be back for dinner."

Caleb smiled again and bolted out the door. A second later he reappeared in the door frame. "I love you, Maw!"

"I love you, too, Son," Alice answered softly, but Caleb was already gone.

Caleb ran all the way down the mountain. In spite of the pre-dawn chill, his heart was beating hard from anticipation and his body was over-heated by the exertion of the run; then he stopped short. He realized he must look very unappealing with sweat pouring from his temples and his hair blown back. He began to second-guess the wisdom of this move.

Just outside the general store was a horse trough. As Caleb approached, he saw no horses in sight. Quickly, for the water was cold, Caleb thrust his head into the water, then shook it vigorously to throw off as much water as possible. When he looked up, there was Mr. Compton, the store owner, standing in the doorway, broom in hand, and eyes wide in confusion.

"Caleb Maghee," he said, "I believe you done took leave of your senses."

"Yes, Sir, I reckon so," Caleb replied with a grin, and commenced the short walk down the street to the apothecary shop that was owned by Grayson Norton. There were lamps lit inside, so Caleb opened the door and walked nervously inside. He had been in the shop before with Callalily, but today, alone and with all his nerves on the edge, he saw the place with new eyes. There was a long counter with shelves behind that held various teas, laxative preparations, herbs, liniment, alcohol, and ointments. On the higher shelves were opiates and morphine. There was an acrid odor and Caleb could just barely see Mr. Norton working at his table in the back with something boiling in a glass jar over a flame. He cleared his throat, mostly to get Mr. Norton's attention. It didn't work. He cleared it more loudly and the apothecary turned and looked into the shop.

"Well, Caleb. What can I do for you? Sore throat?"

"Oh, no, Sir, I, uh . . ." he cleared his throat again, this time for nerves.

"Speak up, Boy; what seems to be your ailment?"

"No ailment, Mr. Norton, Sir. I just, well, I want to ask you . . . a question."

"Question? What question?"

Caleb took a deep breath and looked Grayson Norton in the eyes. "I want to marry your daughter, Sir."

"That's not a question."

Caleb felt that now Mr. Norton was just being obtuse to torture him. "No, Sir, it isn't. My question is . . . may I have your permission to ask Callalily to marry me, Sir?"

"Hmmmmmmm . . . marriage is a serious thing, Boy."

"Yes, Sir, it is."

"If I say yes, how do you plan to take care of my daughter?" Mr. Norton was frowning his most serious frown and Caleb was a little taken aback.

"Sir, I plan to be a writer—a newspaper writer, in Nashville or Memphis. I'm a good writer, Sir."

"Yes, with your education, I imagine you are. Your family has a successful farm on the mountain. You don't plan to stay and help them run it?"

Caleb was beginning to get his footing in this duel of words. "Mr. Norton, my family does have a successful farm, and I have learned how to do just about every kind of work up there. I'm grateful for them and for the opportunity they gave me to go to school as long as I could. Sometimes God just has something else in mind for a man. Mr. Adams will tell you that I have been a good student and that my writing ability is above average, even accomplished. If there was a local paper in Big Bear, I would apprentice there, but there's not, so I will do it somewhere else. I love your daughter and she loves me. I will take care of her wherever we go, and . . . (Caleb had to think hard before he said the last part) if you will give us your permission to be pledged, we won't have the wedding until I am gainfully employed. I love Callalily and I would not see her go without."

"Spoken like a man, Son!" Mr. Norton clapped Caleb on the back. "You have my permission to be *pledged* until you are able to take care of Callie."

"Thank you, Mr. Norton!" Caleb beamed.

"Well, what are you waiting for? Go ask her!"

Caleb rushed out to do just that.

It was still early morning as Caleb headed toward the Norton home. A heavy mist hung over Big Bear Creek and blotted out the face of the sun, but took on its golden glow. The silver frost still clung to fields, trees and rooftops. It seemed a magic world of clouds tipped in pink and amber as the sun climbed, just like Caleb pictured heaven. He did not feel the November chill. The door to the house opened, and there she was, the angel of his heart, basket of bread under her arm to take over to the general store for sale. She was dressed in blue gingham with a crocheted blue shawl over her hair and shoulders. Caleb was too enchanted to speak.

"Why Caleb Maghee, what are you doin' here at this hour?"

"I . . . I came to talk to you," he stammered as he took the basket from her arm.

"Talk about what?"

"My, this bread does smell good!"

"You came to talk about bread?"

"No! Of course I didn't come to talk about bread. Why would I be here at this time of the morning if I only wanted to talk about bread?" Nerves made his voice rise.

"Well, you don't have to shout at me! How should I know what you came to talk about?"

"I'm not shouting!" Oh my, this wasn't the way he intended this morning to go at all. A dog was barking. Stitch! As the persistent animal ran up to him, Caleb heard Tad in the distance: "Turtle! Turtle c'mon quick!"

88

Caleb was torn. He turned to Callalily and said quickly, "Callalily Norton, will you pledge to marry me whenever I can afford to take you as my wife?" Callalily, eyes wide with the shock of his blunt proposal could only nod a weak affirmative. It was enough for Caleb. "Good!" He took the ring out of his pocket and slapped it on the palm of her hand. He kissed her hard on the mouth, then sprinted off with the dog, calling over his shoulder, "I'll talk to you later." At that moment, the sun burst out of the clouds and glistened on the silver and aquamarine ring still in the palm of her hand, and the stunned girl could do nothing but wave to Caleb, her newly intended, as he disappeared around the corner.

# Taken

Caleb followed after Stitch until he reached Tad. "What happened?" he asked even as they continued to run toward home.

"It's Jobie! Bounty hunters done picked him up. They took Grampaw, too."

When they arrived at the house, an official-looking man was arguing with Abe. Stitch circled the man and growled. "It's the law, Mr. Maghee," the man was saying. "The boy belongs to Colonel Clarence Fraley from Columbus, Georgia. His maw and baby sister are still on the run. You know what that means, Sir."

"Why do you find it necessary to incarcerate my father, *Sir*?"

"According to the Fugitive Slave Law of 1850, any persons aiding or providing food or shelter to a runaway slave will be sentenced to six months in a federal prison and fined one thousand dollars," the stranger became condescending in response to Abe's tone of voice.

"Jobie came here as a free Negro. He works for me. I don't know anything about his mother and sister. You hinder the work of my farm if you take two of my men," Abe said trying not to show his emotion.

"Don't be a fool, Mr. Maghee. I would arrest you, too if it were not for your wife over there," he said and indicated Alice standing at the door. "Receive that as an act of mercy. Good day to you, Sir." The man mounted his horse and rode off with Stitch running and barking after him.

Abe shot a steely glance in the direction of his sons, then strode to the barn. They followed him, and from outside the doors they could hear him. Abe was not a man to cuss, but the words he was uttering in that moment were not fit to be spoken in front of his children and his wife. Rant over, he raised his eyes to heaven in contrition, and anguished, "What can I do? Just tell me, what can I do?"

Dinner was eaten in silence that night. After Caleb read from the Bible as usual and Tad and Stitch headed off to bed, Abe told his wife that he was going to walk down by the lake for a little while to think.

"Darlin', it's awfully cold. Don't stay too long."

"Maybe the cold air will hep my thinkin' then," he said. He kissed her on the forehead and went out the door.

Alice had been waiting for a private moment with Caleb. Everyone else may have forgotten in the uproar, but she had not. "Hon, how did it go this morning?"

"Mr. Norton gave permission for us to be pledged, but I promised him we wouldn't marry until I found a payin' job."

Alice sighed in what sounded like relief. "And what about Callalily?"

Caleb shrugged his shoulders.

"Son?"

"Well, first we had an argument."

"An argument? Whatever about?"

"About bread."

"Bread?" She was understandably confused.

"Yes Ma'am, it was just a stupid argument that didn't mean anything. I don't know why it happened."

"Did you give her the ring, then?"

"Yes, Ma'am. I asked her right when Tad called for me. She nodded her head."

"C'mere." Alice opened up her arms and gave him a big hug. "Yer gonna make a fine husband, just fine, but one of these times we need to talk about communicatin'."

Caleb didn't answer, but returned the hug. They both went off to bed, if not to sleep.

Meanwhile, Abe agonized as he walked under the half moon and stars that lit the deep blue beyond, his breath hissing out in thin white clouds. He kept whispering the question, "What can I do? What can I do?" Suddenly, a name came back to his mind—Harold Lowery, the attorney from Chattanooga who had come to tell the community about John Bell. He clapped his hands together and raised his eyes to heaven. "Thank you," he whispered, and headed back up the hill. It was neither a promise nor an answer, but it was a direction, and Abe planned to pursue it the very next day.

The breakfast table the next morning seemed very empty without Abel and Jobie. It was usually a place of good-natured banter and mouth stuffing. After Abe made is plans known, there was silence and leftover biscuits and ham. Alice wrapped the leftovers up carefully for Abe to take along with him. She thoughtfully folded and packed his bedroll, his meeting shirt and another pair of socks. Inside the socks she hid the small amount of cash that was kept in the house for emergencies to pay Harold Lowery for his services. Abe hugged his wife good-bye and instructed the boys to take care of their maw and the place, then headed out on the mule into the gray morning. The mild weather of the day before had been replaced by a freezing drizzle.

"The air smells of snow," Alice commented as she sat down in her chair by the fire and picked up her sewing. The boys headed out to do their chores. As she stitched, Alice prayed for the safety of her husband and the success of his mission.

Caleb was nervous, wanting to go to town to make amends with Callalily for his odd proposal. Alice begged him to stay in case the weather got rough, and it was a good thing. By afternoon the drizzle had frozen on the path, the trees, the rooftops, and continued to fall in large, ashen flakes. "The first snow used to be so beautiful," he thought. Caleb was in the habit of silent prayer, but never had he prayed more fervently than during this time as he waited to see Callalily again, begging that he hadn't ruined everything.

Tad spent the afternoon trying to teach Stitch to fetch, a lesson he had attempted often and which always ended in failure. Tad tossed a ball. Stitch walked over to it. Sniffed it. Then sat down next to it and looked at Tad with his dog grin and swished his tail. Tad tossed a stone. Stitch walked over to it. Sniffed it. Then sat down next to it and looked at Tad with his dog grin and swished his tail. Tad tossed a stick. Stitch walked over to it. Sniffed it. Then sat down next to it and looked at Tad with his dog grin and swished his tail. Tad tossed a sock. Stitch walked over to it. Sniffed it. Groaned and didn't sit too close to it, but looked at Tad with his dog grin and swished his tail. Tad tossed a potato. Stitch walked over to it. Sniffed it. Ate it. Then sat down and looked at Tad with his dog grin and swished his tail. Clearly, this lesson wasn't going to go anywhere.

Afternoon faded into evening, the snow continued to fall, and stew and biscuits were served. As the evening dimmed into dark night, Caleb read to them for a while and they went to bed. No one slept.

The next day was identical.

On the third day, the sun came out early, and except for down in the hollows where the sun didn't reach, the snow began to melt. Plump drops fell from the eaves and everyone took a deep breath. The brutal part of winter had not yet arrived.

By noon, Caleb had his mother's permission to go to town. He went straight to the Norton's house and knocked on the door. Petunia, the youngest sister (They were all named after flowers—Callalily, Rose, Daisy, Laurel, and Petunia), opened the door. She was only five years old.

"Hello, Caleb Maghee. Callie says if you come to talk about bread she ain't interested."

Not this again! "You tell Miss Callalily that I am *not* here to talk about bread!"

Petunia closed the door. In a moment she was back. "She says you can come in then. She's in the parlor."

"Thank you very kindly, Miss Petunia," Caleb answered and Petunia giggled. She led him into the sunlit parlor and he stood awkwardly with his hat in his hands. Callalily was indeed there seated on the couch near the fire untangling embroidery thread.

"Won't you have a seat, Mr. Maghee?" Mrs. Norton offered.

"Yes, Ma'am. Thank you." He sat in the chair across from the couch where Callalily sat. She was clad in a beautiful green dress with ruffles on the hem and sleeves and a white apron with yellow and green embroidery tied around her waist, auburn hair shining, blue eyes intent on her work. In agony he realized that she was not wearing the ring.

"May we get you some tea, Mr. Maghee?" Mrs. Norton asked.

"Oh, yes Ma'am. Thank you." Mrs. Norton hustled Petunia before her out of the room. Caleb was grateful. He didn't want to have this conversation in front of anyone else.

"Callalily," he began. She looked up at him through her long lashes, and in spite of herself she could not hold back a smile. He cleared his throat and got down on one knee in front of her. He reached over and took the embroidery thread out of her hands, then held them both in his own. "Callalily, I love you, and I'm sorry about the way this went the last time. I wish you would do me the honor of becoming my wife, as soon as I'm able to get a newspaper writing job like I told your paw."

"Mr. Maghee, I would be proud to be pledged to be your wife."

"Do . . . do you still have the ring I gave you? It was my gramaw's and my maw's. It isn't new. If you want a new one I'll get you one."

"It just so happens I have it right here," she said as she pulled one hand away from his and produced it from the pocket of her apron. "I thought you might want to put it on me yourself." She placed the ring in his hand, and his heart thrilled at her touch. There was a blush on her freckled cheeks, and her enchanting eyes sparkled like stars. With his eyes still on hers, he slipped the ring on her finger, then he gently kissed her hand, remembering with embarrassment the rough kiss he had given her the last time.

"It's beautiful," she whispered, and smiled.

Mrs. Norton and Petunia returned with the tea tray, followed by Rose, Daisy and Laurel. "It looks like y'all may have some news," Mrs. Norton teased as she set down the tray, and they all rushed over to see the ring.

# "Into the Fire"

It would have been Abel's week to bring the Word at Sunday meeting. Although the whole community had heard the gossip about his arrest, no arrangement had been made for a substitute. This occurred to Alice on Friday.

"Caleb, you're gonna have to take yer grampaw's place in the pulpit Sunday."

"Maw, I can't! No, Ma'am! I don't know what to say!"

"You're the man of the house right now, Caleb, with your paw and grampaw away. It's up to you to fulfill your family's obligations, and part of that obligation is preachin'."

"That's not fair," Caleb replied.

"I know, Darlin'. But just be thankful it ain't fallin' to yer paw. He's a good man, but talkin' ain't his way." She smiled and kissed him on the cheek. "I have confidence in ye, my little . . ."

"Don't say it," Caleb interrupted his mother.

She only laughed and walked away, leaving him with another dilemma to face. Caleb bundled up and set off for the Jemison home where Mr. Adams, the schoolmaster, rented a room.

"What do you want to talk about? What's on your mind right now?" Mr. Adams asked after Caleb presented the situation.

"There are a couple of things. First, I just got pledged to Callalily Norton," Caleb blushed as he said it.

"Congratulations! She is a very fine young woman. I wish you both all happiness."

"Thank you, Sir."

"Can you build that into a Sunday message?"

"Probably not, considering most of the people in the meetin' know a lot more about it than I do."

"And you have a second idea?"

"Yes, Sir, but I'm afraid it's goin' to make people mad."

"What is your idea, Caleb?"

"Well, you know the bounty hunters came and took Jobie off a couple days ago. Then they arrested my grampaw for helping him. Those were two men who never did a soul any harm. They were just livin' their lives and doin' what right they could by folks. Jobie even saved my brother's life one time, and almost got himself killed doin' it. I've prayed and I've thought, Mr. Adams. What were they doin' that was so wrong?"

"There are those who would say that you all were the one's doing wrong because you were keeping somebody else's property," Mr. Adams challenged.

"Yes, Sir, there are those who would. I know the Bible says we should obey the law and the Fugitive Slave Law is a *law*, but there are higher laws."

"And what laws would those be."

"Jesus said, 'This is my commandment, that ye love one another.' He also said to 'do unto others as ye would have others do unto you.' I think maybe if folks were treating their slaves the way Jesus said to treat others, there wouldn't be so much need to escape."

"And so you agree with slavery, Caleb?"

"No, Sir, can't say that I do. When the Bible talks about God creating man in His image and likeness, it doesn't say he created some who were any less than that. I think that's where the real problem is, Mr. Adams. It's not in the law or the government, it's in peoples' hearts. We forget that everyone is created in God's image. We forget that we're supposed to love one another."

Mr. Adams' eyes sparked with pride. The pupil had become the teacher. "You know you aren't going to convince everyone, right?"

"Yes, Sir," Caleb sighed, feeling the weight of this assignment upon his shoulders.

"Then God be with you," Mr. Adams smiled. "I'll see you Sunday."

Caleb turned toward the door.

"Caleb."

"Sir?"

"Think like a newspaperman."

"Yes, Sir. Thank you, Mr. Adams."

*Think like a newspaperman*: the words echoed in Caleb's mind. Evidence. Where could he go for evidence? And what evidence could there be that would not be challenged by half the people in Big Bear? He needed witnesses. Then he had an idea.

* * *

Sunday morning dawned bright and cold and crystal clear. It was one of those mornings when it is impossible to be drowsy because the temperature itself was bracing. The beads of refrozen snow clung to trees, bushes, buildings and everything, bouncing sunlight off their surfaces in all directions.

From all over Big Bear, families arrived for Sunday meeting. At the appointed time, Brother Edwards led several hymns, and then, with a slight note of sarcasm in his voice he pronounced, "This morning we are honored to hear a word from young Brother Caleb Maghee who will speak in place of his grandfather who, sadly, is unable to be with us. We will pray that justice has its way and that the elder Brother Maghee will be back in our company soon." He led the congregation in prayer, then walked purposefully to a seat and deposited himself, looking short-changed.

Caleb, as scintillating as the weather, walked to the lectern with his notes. He looked at the people sitting before him— some were frowning, some were doubting, but some seemed sympathetic. He nodded briefly at Callalily, who smiled back, and at his maw, who also smiled back. He began:

"When a newspaper reporter writes a story, one thing he holds in utmost regard is a witness's account. From witnesses, a man can put together fragments of a story, and ultimately put together the truth of a thing. When we search for the truth of God in what our beloved nation is facing today, we need only collect the testimony of witnesses." He held up his Bible.

Several people voiced an "amen" to encourage him.

Caleb continued, "Let us then, from testimonies of witnesses throughout biblical history, put together the truth of the worth of a man."

"The first witness, the prophet Isaiah said: 'Cry aloud, spare not, lift up thy voice like a trumpet, and show my people their transgression and the house of Jacob their sins. Yet they seek me daily, and delight to know my ways, as a nation that did righteousness, and forsook not the ordinance of their God: they ask of me the ordinances of justice; they take delight in approaching to God: Wherefore have we fasted, say they, and thou seest not? Wherefore have we afflicted our soul, and thou takest no knowledge? Behold, in the day of your fast, ye find pleasure, and exact all your labors. Behold, ye fast for strife and debate, and to smite with the fist of wickedness: ye shall not fast as ye do this day, to make your voice to be heard on high. Is it such a fast as I have chosen? A day for a man to afflict his soul? Is it to bow down his head as a bulrush, and to spread sackcloth and ashes under him? Wilt thou call this a fast, and an acceptable day to the Lord?'"

"Amen! Amen!"

Caleb looked up, then continued, "'Is not *this* the fast I have chosen? To loose the bands of wickedness, to undo the heavy burdens, and to let the oppressed go free, and that ye break every yoke? Is it not to deal thy bread to the hungry, and that thou bring the poor that are cast out into thy house? When thou seest the naked, that thou cover him; and that thou hide not thyself from thine own flesh?

'Then shall thy light break forth as the morning, and thine health shall spring forth speedily: and thy righteousness shall go before thee: the glory of the Lord shall be thy rear guard.'"

There were some whispers of, "What is he talking about?"

"Shall we then ask another witness, the psalmist David? 'God standeth in the congregation of the mighty; he judgeth among the gods. How long will ye judge unjustly, and accept the persons of the wicked? Defend the poor and fatherless: do justice to the afflicted and needy. Deliver the poor and needy: rid them out of the hand of the wicked. They know not, neither will they understand; they walk on in darkness: all the foundations of the earth are out of course.'"

There were no "amens," but Caleb had everyone's attention. One could nearly hear a breath.

"These are wise men, but they are men from a time before our blessed Lord and Savior, Jesus Christ. Let us hear a witness from another time, the Apostle Paul. 'Is the law then against the promises of God? God forbid, for if there had been a law given which could have given life, verily righteousness should have been by the law. But the scripture hath concluded all under sin, that the promise by faith of Jesus Christ might be given to them that believe. But before faith came, we were kept under the law, shut up unto the faith which should afterwards be revealed. Wherefore the law was our schoolmaster to bring us unto Christ, that we might be justified by faith. But after that faith has come, we are no longer under a schoolmaster. For ye are all children of God by faith in Christ Jesus. For as many of you as have been baptized into Christ have put on Christ. There is neither Jew nor Greek, there is neither bond nor free, there is neither male nor female: for ye are all one in Christ Jesus.'

"And shall we then refer to the greatest witness of all, Jesus Christ the Lord, who Himself testified, 'Blessed are the poor in spirit, for theirs is the kingdom of heaven. Blessed are they that mourn, for they shall be comforted. Blessed are the meek, for they shall inherit the earth. Blessed are they which do hunger and thirst after righteousness, for they shall be filled. Blessed are the merciful, for they shall obtain mercy. Blessed are the pure in heart, for they shall see God. Blessed are the peacemakers, for they shall be called the children of God. Blessed are they which are persecuted for righteousness sake, for theirs is the kingdom of heaven. Blessed are ye when men shall persecute and revile you, and say all manner of evil against you falsely for my sake. Rejoice, and be exceeding glad: for great is your reward in heaven.'

"Again, the blessed Savior Jesus instructs us to 'Love the Lord thy God with all thy heart and all thy soul and all thy strength and with all thy mind, and thy neighbor as thyself.' And when asked, 'Who is my neighbor,' He replied with a story:

"'A certain man went down from Jerusalem to Jericho, and fell among thieves, which stripped him of his raiment, and wounded him, and departed, leaving him half dead. And by chance there came down a certain priest that way; and when he saw him, he passed by on the other side. And likewise a Levite, when he was at the place, came and looked on him, and passed by on the other side. But a certain Samaritan, as he journeyed, came where he was: and when he saw him, he had compassion on him. And went to him, and bound up his wounds, pouring oil and wine, and set him on his own beast, and brought him to an inn, and took care of him. And on the morrow when he departed, he took out two pence, and gave them to the host, and said unto him, Take care of him: and whatsoever thou spendest more, when I come again, I will repay thee.'

"'Which now of these three, thinkest thou, was neighbor unto him that fell among thieves?' And he said, 'He that showed mercy on him.' Then said Jesus unto him, 'Go, and do thou likewise.'"

Caleb looked up at the assembly of his friends and acquaintances. He looked several of them in the eye, and repeated just those last words of the scripture: "Go, *thou*, and do likewise." Then he stepped away from the lectern and returned to his seat.

"Amen!" shouted one old-timer from the back of the assembly. Then "Amen! Amen! Yes, Amen!" from others, but not all. Several looked sullen, even angry. Some shook their heads. "Amen!" Came a familiar voice from the door. Abe was home. Brother Edwards walked to the podium to offer a closing prayer.

Out in the yard a few people stopped to congratulate Caleb. One of them was Brother Hugh. "That was a fine message, Son; a fine message."

Mr. Adams said, "You did it, Caleb. You listened to the witnesses and made your report."

Another said, "That was right clever, Boy! They cain't argue with the word of God!—hehehe!

Of course, Alice, Abe, Tad and Callalily and all the Nortons said how proud they were.

"What news on Grampaw, Paw?" Caleb asked when he could get a word in.

"I talked to Mr. Lowery, finally. It was hard to git in to see 'im. He promised he would do what was possible. Guess that's all I could ask."

"What about Jobie. Will he git him back, too, Paw?" Tad was as concerned about his blood brother as he was about his grandfather.

"No, Son. Jobie was sent back to Colonel Fraley. There's nothing anyone can do about that. It's law."

# Then Came December

The usual joy of the Christmas season was dampened considerably that year without Abel and Jobie. The family went through the motions, but it was impossible to feel the warmth and security that had always been there before. However, amidst their dark moods there were two candles that glowed warm and promising—Alice's coming baby, and Callalily.

Mrs. Norton insisted that Callie come up the hill each day to help Alice as she got closer to her time. The woman and the girl began to form an intimate bond based on their common love for Caleb. Alice told Callie stories about Caleb as a child, and the two could often be heard laughing as they cooked together, sewed together, and cleaned together. Without pushing, Alice was passing the family traditions on to the next generation, and Callie was an enthusiastic pupil.

Abe and Caleb were both happy with the arrangement. Abe was concerned about his wife. It had been a long time since she delivered a baby, and she seemed more frail this time than she had before; carrying the weight of the child seemed more difficult. He watched her as she pressed her hands to her back after standing for a while and how she struggled to get out of bed on the cold mornings. Callie's help enabled her to rest and to avoid the heavy part of the work Alice was forced to be responsible for in the absence of Abel and Jobie, especially since it took all Abe, Caleb and Tad could do to keep up with the farm chores. Caleb, of course, was just happy to have her around. Watching her go easily and good-naturedly through the everyday chores of the home, he could picture the good wife she would be.

One evening, as Caleb walked Callie home, he noticed an unusual commotion at the General Store. He saw her to her door, said good-night, and went over to find out what it was all about. Newspapers had arrived! Caleb picked one up and raced for home.

"Maw! Paw! South Carolina has seceded from the Union!" He read aloud to them from the paper: "As concern rises over the role of the Federal Government of the United States under the leadership of President Abraham Lincoln, South Carolina finds itself at odds over the Republican North's opposition to expansion of, and eventual abolition of, slavery in the United States. Tariffs issued to protect the interests of Northern manufacturers along with increased prices for goods sold to the South have added to the tensions. In view of such, South Carolina declares itself free and independent of all concerns arising from that government, and declares itself to be independent." He looked up into the startled faces of his family.

"And so it's begun," Abe said sadly.

"And so it's begun!" Tad responded enthusiastically, and he stroked the head of his dog.

The reality was there in black and white, but South Carolina and secession and war seemed very far away—to everyone but Tad.

A few days before Christmas, Abe brought in a fresh pine tree which filled the house with its fragrance. Then he got out the box of carefully packed Nativity figures that the boys and Abel had made. Happily, Alice and Callie decorated, and then spent the rest of the day baking Christmas cakes. When the day had come to a close and Callie was preparing to go home, the woman and the girl stood side-by-side surveying their accomplishments. It was indeed lovely. Alice reached over and took Callie's hand. She smiled, but her eyes glistened with tears. Somehow it seemed to her as though she had just closed a beloved book for the last time.

As Callie prepared to leave on the night before Christmas, she excitedly gathered up the rag dolls that she and Alice had labored over for her sisters, and Alice wrapped up one of the sweet, heavily spiced apple and raisin cakes for her to take to her mother and father as thanks for allowing their daughter to keep company with an "old pregnant woman." Caleb placed her shawl over her shoulders and took the bundles out of her arms.

"I'll carry these for you, Miss Callie."

"Why, thank you, Caleb. Merry Christmas, Mrs. Maghee, Mr. Maghee, Tad, and you, too, Stitch. I'll be spendin' tomorrow with my family, but I'll see y'all soon!" They all hugged her, which was not their practice, but they did it because it was Christmas and because by then she seemed like one of the family.

When they got to the Norton house, Caleb agreed to come in long enough to deliver the cake along with his parents' best wishes, and to have a glass of punch with the family. It was a happy moment as Grayson Norton toasted Caleb's health and prosperity, his family, his eventual success as a writer, and his very eventual union to Callalily. Mr. Norton refilled his glass for every toast, while Caleb stayed with one, knowing he had to walk home. Still, he was feeling a little dizzy as Callie walked with him back to the porch.

"I have a present for you, Caleb," she said as she handed him a parcel wrapped in paper. "Open it! I made it myself!"

Caleb opened the parcel which contained a very long, red, knitted scarf. "It's beautiful, Miss Callie! Thank you! I really needed one," Caleb said, smiling as he wrapped it twice around his neck. "I have one for you, too." He pulled a small string pouch out of his pocket.

Callie jumped up and down a little. She opened the pouch and drew out several long, blue, satin ribbons. "Oh! They are just lovely!"

Caleb smiled at her enthusiasm. "I thought they'd look nice in your hair." He dared to allow himself to touch her hair very gently.

Closing her eyes, Callie put her arms around his neck and kissed him softly on the lips. "Merry Christmas, Caleb," she whispered.

As Caleb descended the porch steps, he was very dizzy indeed, but it had nothing to do with the punch. He made his way home slowly, savoring the memory of the evening and of the kiss.

When he got home, Alice was standing beside the Nativity set that he and Tad and Abel had made years before. She ran her finger lightly over the blue angel and Caleb knew she was thinking about Abel. When Alice saw Caleb watching her, she picked up the family Bible and carried it to him and asked him to read from the book of Luke, chapter two, the story of the birth of Jesus. Alice smiled as she always did when he read the scriptures, and when he finished, she kissed him good night. "Merry Christmas, Son." Then she walked over to Tad and kissed him, as well. "Merry Christmas, Baby Boy." She patted Stitch on the head and he licked her hand. Abe also said good night.

"Merry Christmas, Maw. Merry Christmas, Paw," Caleb responded.

"Merry Christmas, Maw, Paw," Tad also responded. Then he turned to his brother. "Turtle (Tad had never stopped calling him that), do you think war is going to come, between North and South, I mean?"

"It may happen, Tad. Maybe before too long. There's already talk about secession in Georgia, Alabama, Mississippi, Louisiana, Florida and Texas."

"When it does, guess I'll be headin' North. Good night, Turtle."

"Good night, Tad."

It was late, but Caleb was not sleepy. His brother's remark troubled him and he really missed his grandfather. He decided to walk down to the lake for a while. The full moon was so bright that it lit up the frozen hillside. It was easy to imagine himself on the slopes of Bethlehem. *They were concerned about a government imposing law and taxes on them as well*, he thought ironically. Out loud, Caleb spoke to the jewel-studded winter sky, "The North is not Rome, but this sure feels like the Promised Land. How can we save it, Lord?"

A spring breeze blew out of somewhere in his memory, and in his mind Caleb heard the words, "Carry my tears." Then from across the lake, clear in the moonlight, Caleb saw the figure of a man. He limped slowly down the path, but even from that distance, and in spite of the limp, Caleb knew that figure!

"Grampaw!" He took off like a shot toward the old man.

"Turtle!" his grandfather tried to run, but he was very weak.

Caleb reached him quickly. He pulled off his own buckskin jacket and the new, long, red scarf and put them on his grandfather and gave him a giant hug, just like he used to when he was a boy. "Grampaw! How did you get here? When did they let you go?"

"Seems like that man Lowery convinced the court that I needed to be home. He told 'em ma family couldn't run the farm without me. I said, 'I told ye that the day ye brung me in.' Then they jus' let me go."

"We need to get you inside where it's warm. C'mon Grampaw. I'll help you."

Stitch was already barking at the door when the two walked in. "Maw! Paw! Wake up!" Tad came in rubbing sleep out of his eyes to see why Stitch was barking.

Oh, what a reunion took place in that home on Christmas 1860, early, early in the morning! They stirred up the fire and got Abel seated beside it. A bowl of steaming water with healing herbs was placed before him to soak his blistered and bleeding feet. Food was warmed and put in his hands. For a while, the old man was speechless, but his eyes glistened with tears. When he did speak, it was only two words: "My family!" and then he broke down and cried. Alice, Abe, Caleb, Tad and Stitch all huddled around him and hugged and soothed him, and when he was calm and ready to sleep, his grandsons helped him on to his bed where he slept away the weeks of separation and pain.

Once Abel was finally settled, and Alice was comfortably tucked in, and Stitch and the boys had gone off to sleep, Abe walked silently back to the tree by the window, and amidst new-sewn shirts, hand crocheted scarves, rifle shells, and oranges, nuts, and rock sugar candy, Abe slipped in one more gift—a bottle of excellent Tennessee corn whiskey.

# 1861

In January, word came to Big Bear Mountain that Mississippi, Florida, Alabama, Georgia and Louisiana had seceded from the Union. After several conversations with Abel about his confinement in the prison and the last he saw of Jobie, Tad was ready to go North to join any regiment that would take him. Timmy Crowder, Caleb's old schoolmate was also ready to go and they began making plans to leave together. Then one morning in early February, a personal tragedy greater than Abel and Jobie's shook the family.

Alice had taken to the bed as her time drew near, and on a frozen morning, February 3, 1861, when all the stars in the heavens gleamed brightly in a just silvering dawn, her labor pains began. Callalily, and her mother who had often served as midwife, were sent for. The men waited, alternately praying and pacing around the room, as the women worked to bring little Joshua, pink, robust and healthy, into the world. When he was clean and swaddled the men were allowed in to take a peek.

Alice was exhausted, but obviously thrilled. "Another son, Abe," she whispered in awe. "Ain't he beautiful?"

Abe kissed his wife on her sweat-soaked hair and smiled. "He sure is." Alice reached the bundle up to him and Abe held his youngest son for the first time. He turned to Abel, Caleb and Tad and pronounced, "Joshua."

Mrs. Norton and Callie were thanked over and over, and then left the family to become acquainted with their newest member. Callie, of course, returned the next day. The household was all in a flutter over meeting the needs of this one tiny human. Caleb did not remember Tad at that stage, so the process was new to both of them. Water had to be fetched and kept boiling all the time. Strange smells invaded their atmosphere. Loud cries happened at all times of the day and night. No one got much rest.

Then on the fourth day, Alice was unwell. Her temperature was high and she had no energy, even to hold little Joshua. Mrs. Norton returned and she and Callie prepared goat's milk for the baby. On the fifth day, Alice burned with fever and shouted at hallucinations. Mr. Norton came with some special herbs to make a tea and others to steam into the air. Nothing seemed to help. By the sixth day, Alice's eyes were glassy and she recognized no one. Abe sat by her bed and held her hand while the others came in from time to time to watch and pray. On the morning of the seventh day, Alice Elizabeth Maghee, most beloved of family and friends, passed away from this earth and into the arms of angels, and her family could find no comfort, except for little Joshua who only knew when he was fed and when he was clean.

At the same time as they washed her body, dressed her in her meeting dress, arranged her hair, and laid her in the casket, many miles away, a reluctant Jefferson Davis stood on the Montgomery state house steps and became the President of the Provisional Government of the Confederate States of America.

\* \* \*

Through the month of February, the Maghee family continued in mourning, doing only those chores that were absolutely necessary. Abe walked to the new grave on the top of the hill every day to be near his beloved. As was his way, he did not speak, but his red eyes and gaunt cheeks showed that he was suffering badly. Care of Joshua went from man to man, all of whom were ill-equipped for the job, and Joshua always made them aware of that fact. Abe held him against his chest every night for warmth and for comfort, but either because he was afraid of rolling over on the baby or because he still grievously missed his wife, Abe did not sleep much. Callie was an invaluable help, but when measles hit her home and they were quarantined she was unable to come for several weeks. The house grew cold, the food was sloppily prepared, and the washing went undone.

One day Abel mentioned the idea of hiring someone to help. "Abe, we really don't have a choice. The young'un has needs and we just cain't fill 'em."

"Nobody can fill 'em!" Abe almost spat the words.

"Yer right, yer right; nobody will ever be able to take Alice's place, but dad gum it, Son, you gotta think logical! If we're a-gonna run the farm and clean the house and cook, somebody's gotta take care o' that baby!"

Abe nodded. His father was right, but it still hurt. He took off the next day by himself with a significant amount of the household money. When he returned he brought a young Negro woman with him. When the rest of the family came in that evening, they found dinner cooked and on the table, the house put right, and the young woman sitting in the rocking chair holding Joshua and singing a quiet lullaby.

"This here's Mary. Make her welcome," Abe announced matter-of-factly. Stitch walked slowly up to her, sniffed her, and licked her hand. Then he wagged his tail and returned to Tad. No one else said a word.

After dinner, Abel pulled Abe aside and asked, "Abe, have ye lost yer dern mind? You know what happened last time! I ain't ready fer no more trouble."

"There won't be any trouble this time," Abe responded, but it was all he was willing to say.

Mary was a gentle girl with huge, innocent, dark eyes, cinnamon-colored skin, and a sweet, small smile. Her hair was always tied back in a white scarf, but when wisps of it escaped around her face, one could see that it was black as moonless midnight. She rarely said anything to anyone other than, "Yes, Sir," or "No, Sir," except to little Joshua. She talked to him all the time, and he responded to her with smiles and coos and loving looks. When Callie returned, after the shock of seeing

Mary for the first time, the two young women got along quite well. Callie, who was also still grieving over the loss of the woman she had come to love, was grateful not to have to shoulder the housework, cooking, and care of Joshua alone. They divided up the chores, played together with the baby, and Callie even brought a few dresses over to give to Mary. They worked together in a way that resembled a carefully choreographed ballet, Callie seeing to the cleaning, Mary seeing to the cooking, and both of them joyfully sharing in the raising of baby Joshua.

The routine of the farm began to return to something that resembled normal. Spring came, and violets grew on the grave of Alice Maghee.

\* \* \*

In the rest of the country, things were far from normal. Texas had already made the decision to secede, while Arkansas, Kentucky, and Tennessee awaited the decisions from North Carolina and Virginia. Tennessee had remained, for the most part, pro-Union, until on April 12, Confederate artillery fired on Fort Sumter in Charleston Harbor, South Carolina. Following that attack, President Lincoln called for seventy-five thousand volunteers to end the Southern rebellion. Virginia, Arkansas and North Carolina refused to take up arms against their Southern brothers. Finally, in June, *The Nashville Patriot* printed, "Tennessee waves any opinion as to the abstract doctrine of secession, but asserts the right, as a free and independent people, to alter, reform, or abolish our state's form of government in such manner as we think proper." Before the end of the month, Tennessee was a part of the Confederate States of America.

One morning, as darkness still blanketed the mountains, something woke Caleb up. It was not a sound, it was just a *feeling.* "Tad," he whispered. The darkness did not reply. "Tad, you alright?" Still no answer. Caleb opened his eyes and looked at his brother's bed. It was empty, but there was something on top of the cover—a piece of paper. Caleb picked it up and carried it out into the kitchen. He stirred up the coals in the fire until they jumped to create a small flame.

By the firelight he read:

Dear Paw, Grampaw and Caleb.

Timmy Crowder and me have been planning to go to be solgers for a while. I want to find Jobie and help end the wikedness of slavery. Pray for me and I will pray for you.

Tad

Caleb walked to the door and out into the night. Down near the lake he saw his brother and Stitch. Tad saw him approaching: "I cain't git this dawg to leave me alone, Turtle. Call 'im back, will ye."

"Tad! What are you doing? Don't you think this family has been through enough lately without you breaking Paw's heart, too?" *And mine*, he thought, but didn't say it.

"I have to, Turtle. For Jobie. For Tennessee. I have to go and fight."

"You're no soldier. Neither is Timmy. We need you here. This place doesn't run itself! It takes all of us, and you know that or you wouldn't be sneaking out in the middle of the night!"

"The farm will be fine. Besides, yer not gonna stay. Yer goin' to Nashville or Memphis to write fer a newspaper, or did ye fergit about that? Just because you have so much dern education don't mean nobody else kin help this country!"

"And what if you get killed out there . . . ?"

"Then at least I won't have to hear about the great Caleb Maghee anymore! Good at ever'thing! Well, I think yer nothin' but a coward, hidin' behind this farm, and Maw's death, and Callalily, and Joshua, and ever'thing else, to keep from havin' to follow yer big dreams. Yer scairt yer gonna fail!"

Caleb was stunned. "My brother wouldn't talk that way. You know the Yanks are threatening our way of life, our freedom to live as we choose and govern ourselves. My brother would stay and fight for his *family* before anything else!"

Tad turned to walk away, "Then I guess I ain't yer brother!" That was that. Tad was gone, and Stitch trotted down the road after him.

# Jobie's Journey

Jobie watched wretchedly from the back of a wagon, hands and feet bound in heavy rope. He was shivering, as much from fear as from the cold. Abe was arguing with the three men who had come to serve the slave-owners' justice.

"It's the law, Mr. Maghee," one of the men was telling Abe. "The boy belongs to Colonel Clarence Fraley from Columbus, Georgia. His maw and sister are still on the run."

*No, they ain't,* Jobe thought.

"Why do you find it necessary to incarcerate my father, *Sir*?"

"According to the Fugitive Slave Law of 1850, any persons aiding or providing food or shelter to a runaway slave will be sentenced to six months in a federal prison and fined one thousand dollars," the stranger said.

"Tar-nation, Man! You cain't git no blood from a turnip," Abel retorted, "and if ye think yer gonna hold me up fer six months, ye got another thing a-comin'! That boy is free. He ain't no slave!"

"Shut up, old man!" the man spat. "Git on the horse!"

Abel took a swing at the man, and as Abe ran to his defense, the bounty hunter knocked Abel in the head with the butt of his pistol and he collapsed onto the ground. Then he turned on Abe. "The only reason we ain't takin' you is because of that expectin' woman up there." He tipped his hat to Alice, who was watching but couldn't hear the exchange. "You should be more grateful!" Then indicating the unconscious Abel to the other man, "Tie his hands and feet and toss him in the wagon, too. If he wants to keep company with the darkie, we'll let him."

Jobie was horrified at the lump which was rising on Abel's temple oozing blood. He had seen men beaten before, but never one who was white. The wagon began to move, and Jobie and Abel were driven away from their home and the people who cared about them.

When Abel came around, he seemed very confused. Jobie did his best to explain what had happened, but Abel drifted back into unconsciousness, and Jobie feared for his life. The wagon bumped along the dusty road until dusk. When they stopped for the night, Jobie and Abel were brought a piece of bread and some water, but Abel could not be roused to eat. The next morning, Abel was awake, but he was sick to his stomach and vomited the bread and water that he was given. He seemed to become weaker and weaker.

"I'm awful sorry, Mr. Abel," Jobie spoke quietly to the old man.

Abel couldn't make his mouth speak, so he reached over and squeezed Jobie's hand.

"King Jesus," Jobie whispered, "Come down and hep Mr. Abel. He a good man."

When they reached the first of their destinations, Abel's feet were untied and he was ordered to exit the wagon. Weak and dehydrated, he was unable to stand, so one of the rough men threw him over his shoulder and toted him into a building that had bars on the windows. All Jobie could do was sit and watch, and although he could not let the men see him cry, his eyes misted up. Moments later the wagon lurched forward toward Georgia.

Along the way, three other escaped slaves were picked up. One was huge and very dark. Instead of rope, that man was held in chains—apparently he was dangerous. The bounty hunters referred to him as "the bear." He did not speak much. The other two slaves were smaller but hard work had made them both muscular. Their names were John Simon and John Craver. They whispered back and forth a lot and studied Jobie in a way that made him uncomfortable. They were also tied up tight.

That night, John Simon proposed a plan. "You! Boy!" he said to get Jobie's attention.

"Name Jobie. I ain't a boy."

"A'right, a'right, then, lil *man*."

"Heh-heh," laughed John Craver.

John Simon resumed, "You smaller than us, and those ropes 'roun' yo wrist ain't so tight. If you don' eat nothing, and 'specially not drink nothing fo' a day or two, you'll shrink up 'til you can pull right out of 'em."

"Yeah, what good'll that do?"

"Y'all quit flappin' yer gums!" one of the bounty hunters said.

John Simon made a face that told Jobie to be quiet.

It was a long time afterwards when John Simon resumed the conversation. "When a *man* (he stressed the word) don't eat or drink fo' while, he shrink up some. Bet ye could slip on out 'em . . ."

Jobie did not answer, but the next few times they were offered water and bread, he only pretended to eat and drink to avoid any suspicion. John Simon caught his attention and smiled ever so slightly. John Craver nodded at him. "The bear" said nothing and did nothing.

On the third night, the bounty hunters indicated that they would arrive at their destination the next day. They poked fun at their captives more than usual that night, then went over to the fire to eat. After their dinner, the man who seemed to be in charge pulled out a bottle. Jobie looked at the others. Their eyes were shining.

"Yes, Sir. Have that drink," John Simon whispered.

After a while, all three of the bounty hunters were snoring.

John Simon gave a nod and Jobie, weak but determined, worked his hands free of the ropes which, as John Simon had predicted, had loosened considerably. His feet were more difficult to maneuver out and they chafed and blistered against the ropes, but eventually, he pulled them free as well.

John Simon whispered, "Now get the knife."

Jobie's head was spinning from hunger and dehydration, and he wobbled a little as he stood, but forcing his body to succumb to the discipline of his mind, he moved silently toward the man with the knife on his belt. A break: his belt lay on the ground beside his sleeping frame. Jobie slipped along the ground noiselessly as the men continued to snore. He grabbed the knife and the belt buckle clinked slightly. It sounded like shattering glass to Jobie. He froze. No movement. Off he raced as quickly as he dared back to the wagon. He went first to John Simon, and his hand shook as he cut the ropes. As John Simon tried to free himself from the web, Jobie moved toward John Craver. The world seemed to be moving beneath him, heaving up and down. John Simon caught him as he fell and lowered him to the wagon bed. It was John Simon who then cut John Craver's bonds. Then he looked helplessly at "the bear" in his chains. Suddenly, the great, huge, silent man, flexed his muscles and exerted all his strength against the chains. Snap! Rings came apart and his arms were free. John Craver grabbed a pry bar from the front of the wagon, and helped "the bear" out of his leg chains, although the heavy rings around his ankles remained, he could walk and run. All this took place in a matter of moments. As "the bear" leaped from the wagon, he grabbed Jobie and threw him over his shoulder like a cotton sack and they all made off for the woods while their former guards slept without a clue.

Even with his burden, "the bear" took the lead as they ran through the woods. He seemed to have a sense of where he was going so the others followed. Near dawn they walked through a hollow that enlarged to what might be considered a small gorge. A muddy stream struggled through it, slipping over smooth rocks and red clay. Above, iron gray clouds were rolling in and the wind was beginning to pick up. "The bear" slowed and looked around. He had apparently found what he was searching for. He pulled back some thick, dry brush to reveal the entrance to a cave. He ducked in carrying Jobie and the others followed. To their amazement there were two more people inside. "The bear" addressed them, his voice deep and strong, though not loud, "We need to get to Moses."

"It won't be today," one of the people said. "Storm's a-comin'."

"What's wrong with that 'un?" the other asked.

"Needs somethin' to eat and drink."

"We all do," John Simon said.

"Hep yo'self," they indicated a pot of some kind of stew. It was cold. "Too dangerous to start a fire out here. We'll move y'all along tomorra."

After some water, administered in sips, and some of the stew, Jobie came back to normal. Of course, he was full of questions. He had not achieved the patience that comes when long periods of suffering and maltreatment couple with an elusive hope that winks its eye from time to time. On his feet again, Jobie was restless.

"Boy!" one of the strangers cautioned, but Jobie moved the brush to step outside. Instantly, the wind snatched the brush away. Rust-colored dust blew down through the gorge, catching him unaware. It stung his face and filled his eyes and nose. Jobie retreated back into the cave and spat the dirt out of his mouth. When he turned to face the others, they returned first expressions of shock and then uncontrollable laughter. They howled; they hooted; they laughed until they ached. Even the silent "bear" laughed until his eyes filled with tears. And Jobie stood there completely clueless until one of the strangers who was dressed in a man's clothing but turned out to be a woman brought him a rag.

"Wipe yo' face down, Boy! You looks mo' like a Injun than a Negro."

Jobie took the rag and wiped it across his face. Red dirt had indeed plastered itself all over him. His clothes were also covered.

"I done needed a laugh. It been a looong time, a looooong time . . ." the woman said still chuckling.

At that moment there was a roar like the sound of an approaching locomotive that echoed through the hollow, and the deluge began. All six dashed to the very back of the cave, which was not that deep, and huddled together to stay warm and dry. The wind made maniacal howling noises and the trees waved in a frantic dance. Then in the middle of the storm, the woman began to sing:

> "O stan' yo' storm, O stan' yo' storm, O stan' yo' storm
>    Till de win' blows over.
> Stan' yo' storm, stan' yo storm
>    Till Jesus sets you free.

(The others joined her.)

Hail, hail, belieber hail;
    Hail from de udder shore.
Hail, hail belieber;
    Yo' times gwine by-o."

They sang together, clapping their hands to the rhythm of the song, until the storm had passed and golden beams of sunlight pierced the clouds.

"Y'all git some sleep. We headin' out at dark," the man told them as he and John Simon gathered some fallen branches together to recover the entrance to the cave, careful not to leave footprints in the clay.

As they settled into as comfortable positions as they could achieve, Jobie asked "the bear," "What yo' name? I know it ain't really Bear."

"Tom," the deep voice answered.

"Tom. Thank you fer gitten me here safe. I'm Jobie."

"Hey, Jobie." And that was that.

After dark they started the long walk to "Moses," and by dawn they arrived at a large plantation. They were led up to a house, although not the main house, behind some brambles, and through a low doorway that led into a crawl space. Through the narrow spaces between the rough-cut floorboards, Jobie could just make out that they were in a carriage house. Another smaller door opened and the four men crawled into the cramped, windowless back room of the carriage house. The man and woman from the cave, whose names they never knew, had disappeared. An elderly white couple had taken their place. There was food and clean water brought in, and amid the clutter of wheels, horseshoes, carriage parts, and other stored items, the men were made comfortable.

"Tom!" the elderly woman exclaimed quietly, patting the big man on the back. He reached down and hugged her. She was a small woman anyway, but Tom made her look like a child.

"Where Moses?" he asked.

"Soon," she nearly whispered back. The woman patted Jobie on the arm and smiled a kind smile. Then the couple left. Boxes were stacked over the doorway where they had entered, and they piled them in front of the other door as well. Jobie washed the best he could, then ate. He felt better than he had since he left Big Bear, even in the stuffy, crowded room. He drifted off into a long, peaceful sleep, but was awakened just after dusk by a slight tap at the small hidden door.

Tom put his finger to his lips, and they all waited. About a minute later, there was another tap. Still they waited. Then they heard tap-tap . . . tap-tap . . . tap-tap, and Tom moved the boxes away from the door.

An old Negro woman and a man in buckskin came through the small door. Her eyes shone. "Tom," you've done it again, Gawd bless you."

"Almost didn't make it this time," Tom answered.

"But Gawd was watchin' over you!" She greeted the others with a smile. "Y'all ready to take freedom?"

"Yes,"

"Yes, Ma'am."

"We ready."

"As soon as it's dark, then. This is your guide," she said and indicated the man in buckskin. He was dark-skinned, but he was not a Negro. Even in the subdued light, his eyes appeared brilliant green. The guide tipped his hat and went back outside to wait.

"Is that Moses?" Jobie asked.

"This here Moses," Tom said indicating the woman.

"My name is Harriet, Son. Some people call me Moses. I reckon it's because I done like he did—lef' my family and friends and followed the Lawd; and now, I he'ps His people to freedom." She patted Jobie's hand and he felt like he had been touched by an angel.

After dark, the tapping came at the small door again. Silently they stole out into the night. The green-eyed man in buckskin met them at the wood line, and John Simon, John Craver, Jobie and he started off with enough food in packs for several days. Suddenly, Jobie realized that Tom was not with them. He turned to see him, a big bear of a man standing in the twilight at the edge of the wood, waving his hand in farewell. Jobie waved as well, then turned so as not to lose track of the rest of the company. They were moving quickly. When he turned to look at his friend one last time, Tom was gone.

The trek was indeed a fast one, resting during the heat of the day, and running the rest of the time. During one of their rest stops, as John Simon and John Craver slept soundly under the leaves, Jobie walked over to speak to their guide.

"I feels like I know ye, Sir."

The guide smiled. *You should be resting.*

"I s'pose so. Where we headed?"

*Canada.*

"Are we close?"

*Not yet.*

"Do ye know where we are?"

*Philadelphia.*

"Philadelphy! Yeah! Can I ask you somethin'?

*Of course.*

"Where can I join the Yanks?"

*Is that what you want to do?*

"Yes, Sir. I gotta family back in Tennessee, not ma real family, a white family. They was awful good to me. Mr. Abel, the grampaw, he done gut taken away too, put in jail 'cause o' me, 'cause they 'lowed me to live wit 'em. When I was little, my maw run away with me and my baby sista 'cause they done sold away the res' of our family and they was fixin' to sell us away from each other, too. The bounty hunters come after us. They shot ma maw. Then this man come and take us to . . . You! It was you! You told me to . . . to . . ."

*Carry my tears.*

"Yes!"

*To bring good tidings to the meek; to bind up the brokenhearted; to proclaim liberty to the captives; and to open the prison to them who are bound.*

"Yes! You say, 'Carry my tears,' an I pick up ma sista . . . little Mary . . ."

*You loved her.*

"Yes."

*There's not enough love in the world these days. It's the only power that changes things. Love your neighbor as yourself; love your enemy, as well, Jobie. Carry my tears.*

"Sir, take John Simon and John Craver to Canada. I'm goin' go fight for ma family!"

# Tad's Journey

Timmy Crowder met Tad at the twin oaks at the foot of the mountain, their arranged meeting place. Timmy did not have his pack or gun with him. As Tad approached, Timmy just stared at the ground.

"Tim?"

"I talked to ma paw last night. I know we was gonna keep our goin' a secret, but I just couldn't leave without sayin' goodbye to my paw. He counts on me Tad. Ye have to understand. He ain't well. He suffers terrible from the gout, 'specially this time o' year. I jus' cain't leave 'im to work the saw mill alone."

"Timmy, we talked 'bout this! We was goin' together, to fight for the cause of those who cain't fight for theirselves."

"I know, Tad; I know. But Paw needs me and my mind is made up. I cain't go."

"Well, I'm a-goin'!" Tad was angry. First Turtle tried to stand in his way, now this. He turned and walked quickly away, and he didn't acknowledge the apology that Timmy called after him. Stitch whined, but padded along beside him. By the time the sky was full-light, Tad was well on his way. The plan was to follow Big Bear Creek to the Tennessee River, then to follow the river which would take him south for a while, then turn north to the first town where he could enlist as a soldier in the Union army. From there he would go where the officers led him. The plan had not been to be alone in the travelling, so Tad was somewhat relieved that Stitch had been so loyal.

Standing on a rock ledge above the river that evening, Tad was overwhelmed by the beauty of the Tennessee sky, bright red and orange, like fire rising from the mountains. Fir and spruce trees reached like church steeples in black silhouette against the brilliance of the sunset. He lowered his pack from his shoulder and watched the colors dance until they were replaced by mist, and the horizon blended into the deepening blue of night. "Beautiful Tennessee," he whispered to the twilight, "why did ye choose the way ye did? Is there not enough freedom in all of this for ever'one?" He sighed deeply and settled down for the night as the first stars winked in the heavens.

At dawn, Tad and Stitch ate a bite, then continued the difficult journey. Through the misty valley they walked where the play of sun and shadow turned the landscape from bright yellow to deep green and back again to the melody of the silver-blue river. Tad had confidence in his ability to navigate this trip, but he had not been able to conceive of the distance, nor had he factored in a second mouth (even a canine one), and before long his provisions began to run low. There were towns along the banks of the Tennessee, but to avoid questions Tad kept moving through them, tipping his hat nonchalantly to those he passed. Strangers were common along this route, so he raised little curiosity.

The summer days were very hot, so Tad and Stitch made most of their progress during early morning and late afternoon when the air was cooler and the surrounding hills were smoky and blue. During the intense heat of the days, the two spent some of their time swimming in the river. Those moments reminded Tad of swimming in the lake at home, but there was no catching fish in that rapid current, not by hand at least, so Tad hunted on land to provide his meals. On one blistering afternoon, as they frolicked in the cool water like a boy and a pup, a movement from the shore caught Tad's attention. He looked just in time to see a young man running off into the woods with his pack and his gun. "Hey! Come back here!" he shouted, but of course, the thief did not stop.

They got out of the water and Stitch shook off, propelling water droplets in all directions. So did Tad. "At least they left my clothes behind," he said to the dog. It was no use trying to run down the culprit by that time, so Tad dressed and on they went. The going was easier without the weight of the pack and gun, but Tad had serious questions about how they were going to survive.

They walked the rest of the day, only stopping to sleep. In the morning, Stitch went off to find food. He came back with a rabbit, but Tad had no way to start a fire to cook it, and although he was famished, he did not eat. They rinsed off in the river, then tried to sleep through the heat of day, consuming only water and what edible vegetation they could find.

Venturing deeper into the woods that afternoon, Tad located a patch of wild blackberries which offered some provision, but picking what was on the inside of the bushes was tricky and the thorns made small tears in his shirt. Even under the trees, the river sang to them in crystalline tones that blended with the song of the birds as they walked along. The air was hot, but held a slight moldy scent because of the wetland and that made it seem cooler. On any other occasion, it would have lightened Tad's mood and heightened his sense of adventure, but he was just too hungry. Then, as another evening was falling along with his hope, Tad spotted a welcome sight—smoke from a campfire.

Quickening their pace, Tad and Stitch leaped rocks and fallen logs toward the source of the smoke. Then he saw it! A nice cooking fire with one man, dark of skin and hair, clad in buckskin. He was skewering fish to put over the fire when he saw Tad. *Welcome*, he said in an accent that Tad did not recognize.

"Thanks," Tad replied. "Reckon ye have enough for two? I haven't had much in two days."

*You mean enough for three*, the man said indicating Stitch.

"Yessir, three," Tad was embarrassed. He had never before had to beg for food, brilliant hunter that he was.

*Sit. I am Merea.*

"May . . . ray . . . ?"

*In your language, it means Companion. Please, sit.* Tad's eyes met the clear, emerald green eyes of the man, and he was startled at their depths, at once cool as the river and warm as the fire. They vaguely reminded him of someone, but he couldn't recall whom.

"What are ye doin' out here by yerself?" Tad started a conversation to fill the time while the fish cooked. The aroma of dinner was driving him nearly mad.

*I am a guide and scout. What about you?*

Tad was aware only then of the possibly dangerous situation into which he had put himself and Stitch. If this *Merea—Companion* happened to be an agent for the South, he might decide to kill them in their sleep. He thought as quickly as he could.

"I was out here to hunt. Stitch and I went in the river to cool off, and somebody stole our supplies, bedroll, gun—ever'thing but my clothes."

*Where are you bound, Hunter?* Companion asked, pausing at the improvised name.

"Tad, the name's Tad . . . well, it's Jacob, but ever'body knows me calls me Tad, short fer Tadpole."

Companion smiled a little. *And how do you come by such a name?*

Tad told him the story. Companion chuckled a little. The fish was done and Companion handed him some on a plate with a biscuit beside it. It tasted wonderful and was very satisfying. The cool of dusk had come. Companion tossed a bedroll over to Tad. *Get some rest.*

As much as Tad, in his pride and distrust, wanted to argue about it, he was suddenly just too tired to hold up his head. The fire was warm, the ground was fragrant, his stomach was full, and before long, he was sound asleep, Stitch by his side.

At Dawn, Tad woke with a start. His first thought was that his gun was not beside him. Then, he remembered. Companion seemed not to have moved during the night, yet the fire he presided over held a pot with hot chicory "coffee," and an iron frying pan of potato cakes.

As they ate, Tad found himself talking about home. Companion listened with interest, but made few remarks.

When Tad finally wound down, Companion asked, *You're not really out here to hunt, are you?*

Tad wondered just how he had betrayed himself and answered honestly, "No, Sir. I'm headin' north."

Companion's startling eyes once again met Tad's and Tad had the feeling that it didn't matter what he told this man; he felt he already knew the truth.

*And you intend to . . .*

Tad spoke emphatically to cover his lack of confidence, ". . . enlist in the Union army!"

Companion nodded his head. *It is a long way, but if you like, I will go with you.* And that was that. By the time the mist began to rise and the golden rays of the sun to pierce the thickness of the trees, the three were headed north.

*We'll follow the river*, Companion decided. *It's probably not the fastest way, but it will be the easiest.*

The river way was breathtakingly beautiful. The trees began on the shore and reached all the way to the peeks of the hills. From a distance they looked like green velvet. The sky was bright blue and full of flocks of wooly clouds, playful in the wind. Around noon, the sun was high and hot and Tad and Stitch really wanted to get out into the river. *Go ahead*, Companion said, *I'm going to fish.*

"Wrong time of day for fishin'." Tad laughed and shook his head. He thought, *this man must be greener than he seems if he thinks he's gonna catch much this time of day. I may end up lookin' after him before it's over.* Tad and Stitch jumped into the water and splashed about, forgetting about Companion and his folly. However, when they had finished and were dry and dressed, they walked over to find Companion with a very respectable catch. In fact, fish swarmed in the water close to where he stood.

"That is incredible!" Tad announced.

*Let's clean them up and have a meal*, Companion returned modestly.

"But how did you . . ."

Companion didn't respond. He was already on his way up the bank. However, if Tad could have seen his face, he would have seen him smile.

They lunched, napped, then headed out again. When next they stopped, Companion tossed his rifle to Tad. *Your turn to bring in the meat.* That made Tad unexpectedly proud, to be trusted by this individual, and he did not let Companion down. They had quail for dinner that night.

As Companion cleaned up and they prepared for sleep, Tad asked him, "Where are you from? Ye don't sound like yer from Tennessee."

*I come from a place where there is beauty, and peace, and love. You will see it one day.*

"Beauty we have, but peace and love? You must not be from the North *or* the South."

*I am very far away from home, indeed,* Tad thought he noticed a note of homesickness.

"Are there slaves there?"

*Slaves? No.*

"Then what are you doing here? Are you going to fight for the Union, too?"

*I have come to bring good tidings to the meek; to bind up the broken-hearted; to proclaim liberty to the captives; and to open the prison to them that are bound; to proclaim the acceptable year of the Lord, and the day of vengeance of our God; to comfort all who mourn; to appoint unto them that grieve in the mountain, to give them beauty for ashes, the oil of joy for mourning, and a garment of praise for the spirit of heaviness; that they may be called oaks of righteousness, the planting of the Lord, that He may be glorified.*

Tad was in awe. "Whoooooa! Are you President Lincoln?" he asked.

Companion laughed a deep, joyous laugh and tossed his cleaning rag at Tad.

"Well, are ye?" Tad persisted.

Companion simply shook his head and laughed again.

They continued along the river, through town and forest, heat and rain, for over two hundred miles. Tad felt very comfortable with Companion, although they didn't talk a whole lot. One night, though, Tad opened up to him about his family, about Turtle, about the birth of Joshua and death of his mother, and about Jobie.

*Do you feel in your heart that you have done the right thing?* Companion asked.

"I feel that I've done the only thing I could do."

*And do you trust the One to whom you pray?*

Tad looked up. He wondered how Companion knew that he prayed. He had never made a show of that; never done it out loud. "I trust God."

*Then you must believe that He watches over His sons in all things.*

"You believe in God, then?"

*Yes.* And that was that.

Afterwards, Tad's prayers changed a little. Whatever else his heart prayed, he always said, "I trust you, God. Watch over all yer sons in all things."

One day, they came near a place called Paducah, Kentucky. Several men in blue rode up beside them on horses. Tad got their attention and asked, "Sir, is the Union still lookin' for soldiers?"

"That way," one of the men pointed as they rode by. "Grant's camped just outside Paducah."

"Thank ye, kindly!" Tad turned to Companion. "Did ye hear?"

*It seems you have found what you were seeking.*

"Are you coming, too?"

Companion smiled and tossed Tad the rifle. *You might need that.* Sadly, Tad realized that Companion was saying good-bye.

"Thank ye for all ye done. I think Stitch and I would have had a time gettin' here without ye. Ye know, if ye stay with us, ye could work on settin' them captives free, like ye said."

*Tad, thank you for walking my path with me for a while. I have been glad of your company, and Stitch's,* Companion reached down and stroked the dog's head. *If you ever need me, I won't be far away. Take care, and God go with you.* Companion's emerald green eyes sparkled.

"And with you, Sir."

Tad turned quickly and walked away before he was overcome by some emotion he could not understand. Boldly into the camp he strode and up to a man at a desk. "Where do I sign up?" A book was placed before him and he signed on the line.

"What about the dog?"

"He stays with me."

"That'll be up to yer commander, Son."

By the end of the day, Tad and Stitch had joined the ranks of the Union Army under General Ulysses S. Grant. Tad soon became recognized for his marksmanship. Ammunition was scarce though, so instead of shooting much, the new recruits marched and dug, dug and marched. During the monotony of those activities, Tad's thoughts turned toward home. In the cadence of the steps of the march, he could visualize his mother's sewing needle going in and out with regularity; in the digging of the ditches, he could see the pitch forks as they flung hay into the barn; in the wind he could hear his grandfather's guitar; in the voice of his commander, he heard his father, stern and purposeful; and in the laughter of his comrades, he could hear Turtle and Jobie. How he missed his brother and best friend! How he wished they were with him!

Tad was never as good a student as his brother, but he could read and write adequately, and that made him popular among the soldiers to write letters for them as they dictated, to be sent home to their loved ones. Tad never wrote letters to his own family, though. He somehow felt ashamed to have left them the way he did. He particularly loathed his last words to his brother. Tad didn't know how to work his way through that emotion on paper, so he didn't try.

Stitch was also very popular with the soldiers. They had adopted him as their mascot. As a result, he always had someone to play with and he always had extra rations. At night, though, he found his best friend and listened quietly to Tad as he talked about everything that lay on his heart, helped him to say his prayers, and slept with him on his cot.

Fall came, and the blazing beauty of the hills was a reminder of the hunts at home with Jobie and Turtle. Memories of Jobie always inspired Tad, reminding him why he was there, why he had made the decision to fight for those who could not. The words of Companion came back to him, *to proclaim liberty to the captives.* Yes, that is what he wanted to be a part of.

Then came the winter. It was nearly impossible to get warm in the windy tents. Stitch was a good heater through the nights though, and because of him Tad always slept well. The soldiers chomped at the bit for the glory of battle. During the month of February, several skirmishes took place, and the force of Grant and his troops grew very strong and intimidating. Grant, himself a rather scruffy man as generals went, but very intense, had the ability to drive the best out of every soldier, and Tad, although he had no personal contact with the man, admired him very much.

War changes a person. Tad, the tender-hearted mountain boy was becoming calloused to the sounds of weapons, the smoke of burning buildings, the blood of the enemy, and even the suffering of his comrades. He did not become calloused out of evil, and not even out of the anger that had driven him to serve the Union. He let go of his feelings in self-defense. He was an excellent marksman but he had to block the idea that he was firing upon human beings. Instead, they became a faceless idea, and if they had a name, it was "Johnny Reb."

Grant led his troops on to Fort Donelson. Gunboats arrived on the Cumberland to aid, but because of the position of the fort on a hill, they proved to be at a disadvantage. There were Rebel forces in control of the fort, and they wasted no time in disabling the fleet of vessels on the river. Meanwhile, Union soldiers froze under cover of snow and leaves. Since Grant had gone to confer with General Foote over the condition of the ships, it was General C. F. Smith who finally ordered the Federal soldiers on. "You volunteered to be killed for love of your country—now's your chance!"

The attack raged in wave after blue wave against the Confederate occupied fort. Tad and Stitch were with a group pushing forward when a cannon ball hit close to him propelling debris into the air and shooting a giant rock into Tad's thigh.

Pain like he had never known knocked him to the ground and held him there. Stitch, who had not left his side, lay across his body to protect him as the battle continued all around them. Tad could not feel his leg and feared the blow had taken it off. With that thought in mind, he passed into darkness.

It was hours later when Tad opened his eyes and looked straight into the emerald green eyes of Companion, who was holding a cup of warm broth to his lips. He knew right away that his leg was still there because the pain was incredible.

"Where . . . ?" he tried to talk.

*Rest. You will be fine. Your work isn't finished yet.*

Stitch was licking Tad's hand and trying hard to get to his face, as well.

*Easy, Stitch. You have to be gentle now,* Companion patted his paw soothingly.

"How . . . ?" Tad was still struggling to understand what had brought Companion to his rescue, but it was too difficult to think right now and he was awfully sleepy . . .

When next Tad opened his eyes, he was in the medic's tent.

"How are you feelin', Soldier?" a man asked him as he worked at removing the dressing from Tad's thigh.

"Better, I reckon. Where's Companion?"

"He's right here. Hasn't left your side. Dern good dog!"

"No, Sir, uh, yes, Sir. That's Stitch. He is a good dawg, but I was askin' about Companion . . . Merea . . . the man who brought me in."

"Oh, yes—the young Negro. Told me his name was Jobie and he knew you from home."

"Jobie?" Tad was incredulous.

"That's what he said. He saved your life. They all thought you were dead out there, but the dog brought Jobie to you, and Jobie picked you up and carried you to me. He insisted that you wouldn't give up that easily."

"Jobie!"

The medic was still talking, ". . . I'd say you are one lucky young fella."

"Jobie is here!"

"Been coming in to check on you every day."

"Yer awake!" It was a voice Tad could never have forgotten. Stitch jumped up and greeted his friend at the tent flap.

"Jobie! I cain't believe it!"

Jobie crossed to where Tad lay on the cot amidst the other injured men and clasped his hand. "It's good to see you, Tad."

"How are you here?"

Jobie sat down and told Tad everything, ignoring the sideways glances of the other men who, though they fought for the Union, were not entirely comfortable with this kind of intimacy between the races.

"And what about the family?" Jobie asked.

Tad told him about Abel's return, and about Alice and the baby, but he did not mention the bitterness with which he had left his brother.

"Oh, Miz Alice. Gawd bless 'er." Jobie shook his head, tears in his eyes. After a moment he continued, "They don' let me fight. They calls me *Contraban'*. But they sure does appreciate the way Miz Alice showed me aroun' the co'n bread an' beans."

"What happened at Donelson?" Tad asked intentionally changing the subject.

"The Rebs tried to escape, but they couldn't get out. When General Grant got back, they give 'im a note from the Reb leader askin' 'is terms o' surrender." Jobie chuckled. "Grant say, 'unconditional and immediate surrender,' and the Rebs had no choice."

Tad laughed a little.

"Tad, I gots to admit something'."

"What's that, Jobie?"

"A whiles back we was marchin' through a town. Don't rightly know where. Well, there was this ol' man sittin' on 'is porch and he had a banjo crossed his knee and he was a-playin' 'Dixie.' I knowed it weren't right, but I kindly teared up."

"I know, Jobie. I miss it, too."

"Someday I'm goin go back.

"Jobie!" a man called in.

"'Comin', Jobie responded. Tad, I gots to go. We movin' out. You take care. I hopes to see ye soon. When all this over, we'll go huntin' agin on Big Bear Mountain."

"Take care, Jobie!"

The medic helped Tad to sit up, and then to stand. There was some soreness left in his leg, but he could definitely get back to duty. What did Companion say? *Your work is not finished yet.* Or was that just the result of a fevered mind after his accident? Jobie was not a hallucination though, and for that, Tad was very grateful.

With the Tennessee and Cumberland waterways securely in Union hands, Grant and his Army of the Tennessee were ordered south to meet General Don Carlos Buell and his Army of the Ohio with the intent of penetrating Mississippi. The march was difficult and conditions were less favorable than they had been. The weather was wet and very cold. Rations were limited to beans, bacon, pickled beef and dried vegetable cakes that became a sort of soup when added to boiling water. How Tad missed the love and passion his mother had put into their meals! She could have even made those simple rations special.

Tad recovered completely from his injuries, but inside he had changed. Surrounded only by soldiers, his once tender heart was hardening. Once he desired only to be like his big brother; to replace that ambition, he desired to be like the seasoned soldiers, the ones who seemed to have no fear. He reined in his boyhood emotions. The only thoughts that still touched him were memories of his family, which he tried to keep at bay, and Stitch, the only one with whom he shared his feelings. Encouraged by the fiery Federal soldiers, the seeds of hatred grew inside him. As Tad marched, he felt it in the cadence of his steps, in the sound of his boots as he lifted them over and over out of the icy, sticky mud, and even in the beating of his heart—"I hate Johnny Reb, I hate Johnny Reb . . ." and since he had a wound to avenge, he grew more than ready for another opportunity to unleash that hatred.

One morning, Tad sat having coffee with a group of friends. Suddenly, one of the new boys, son of a wealthy Washington military family who had him assigned by request to Grant's unit, Collin Fields by name, threw his coffee into the air with a brain-piercing squeal.

"What in tarnation?" Tad asked as Stitch gently pushed Collin onto a bench to sit him down before he passed out.

"The coffee was moving!" Collin whimpered, his breath coming in short gasps.

The others looked at each other, then broke out in loud, unsympathetic laughter.

"Did it look like this?" a big, rough fellow named Jeb asked, and put his cup right up under Collin's nose.

Collin looked down and turned green! "Yes! Yes! What is it?"

The others laughed all the more, except for Stitch who licked the boy's hand and tried to comfort him.

"It's just weevils," Tad said, trying to temper his amusement. "They're in the hardtack. They won't hurt ye, but if ye want, ye can just rake 'em off the top and they'll be gone. They don't even taste like nothin'."

Collin gave him a dirty look.

"Oh, Boy," Jeb responded, "you prob'ly done already et a pound of 'em since ye bin here."

"I don't intend to eat insects!" Collin huffed, stood and walked away, wiping Stitch's slobber off his hands with an embroidered handkerchief, the laughter of the men following him.

Two weeks later, the troops headed south. Spring had arrived, and even though that meant a break in temperatures and a much greener landscape, the early spring rains also fell, and when they came during a march, movement was difficult and slow. During the last days of March, the men, horses, mules and wagons struggled down a sunken road and stopped to make camp near Pittsburg Landing, Tennessee. Forty-seven thousand men under the command of General Grant waited for the coming of General Buell and eighteen thousand men. Days went by and the soldiers became restless. Fights broke out for no reason at all. To keep down trouble in the camp, the men were put to digging ditches. Line after line of ditches slashed the countryside near a little white-washed church called Shiloh.

As the wait dragged on, many of the men began having symptoms of illness. Stomach cramps, fever, bloating, and what became known as "the Tennessee two-step," caused weakness and dehydration among even the strongest of the soldiers. For a while, it was treated as a joke until one day the word came—Collin Fields was dead of dysentery. He was not the last.

Meanwhile, only twenty-two miles away, in the little town of Corinth, Mississippi, unknown to Grant and his troops, General Albert Sydney Johnston camped with his amassed Confederate troops forty-five thousand strong.

# Caleb's Journey

Caleb stood there in shock and watched his brother walk away. Never in all his life had Tad spoken that way to anyone, particularly not the big brother he admired and wanted to emulate. As Tad disappeared into the mist of dawn, Caleb forced himself to shake off the sting of Tad's last words, "Then I guess I ain't yer brother." He turned and walked slowly toward home wondering what he would tell their father, but when he arrived, Abe was already holding Tad's note. His hands were shaking, and there was a look of pain on his face.

"Is he gone, Son?"

"Yes, Sir."

"Reckon we best git to work."

Caleb followed his father out to the barn. Behind him, he heard Joshua start to cry, and he saw Mary's shadow as she went to get him. They met Abel limping around the side of the building. "Tar-nation! Those foxes . . . Abe! What's wrong?"

"Tad's gone to fight . . . for the Yanks."

"Tar-nation!"

The foxes were a particular problem that summer, along with an unusual influx of locusts which decimated the corn and young trees. Fortunately, there was some extra put up in the barns for emergencies, but even with the skill of Abel, Abe and Caleb and the resourcefulness of Callie and Mary, food was in short supply. Hunting became more important to survival. Abel kept his hooks wet and brought in a fair amount of fish from the lake, and Abe and Caleb brought in foul and various small game. Even that was harder to come by than usual, since everyone in the area was handling the same problem. Still, neighbors were neighbors, and everyone seemed intent that no one in the community would go hungry.

There were many visitors to the mountain that summer. Mostly, they were people who came to trade what they could for food. Sometimes they were men asking about Tad and about Abel's experience in the prison. Some regarded Tad as a hero and some considered him a traitor. There was also talk about the slave that Abe Maghee had bought for a nanny to baby Joshua. No one else in Big Bear owned a slave, and a few thought the Maghees were just getting too big for their britches.

A day arrived when men in blue rode into town. They had been sent to "occupy this hostile region," and although they claimed only to want to keep the peace, they helped themselves to what they wanted without invitation and without regard for anyone else's needs. Whatever Union sympathies had existed prior to their arrival quickly disappeared. The kind and generous people of Big Bear became suspicious and resentful. There was no fair that fall, no desire to celebrate the conditions in which they found themselves.

Frozen winter came without a glimmer of joy. The faces of the people were gaunt with need and hopelessness. Callie and Mary did their best to bring a bit of cheer into the Maghee home in honor of the birth of Jesus. The treasured Nativity set was brought out and placed in its normal spot in the keeping room, but no tree was brought in to decorate. Their absence was felt every day, but the family had never been so sad as that Christmas without Alice and without Tad.

On Christmas Eve, Caleb read from Luke, chapter two:

"And it came to pass in those days, that there went out a decree from Caesar Augustus that all the world should be taxed. And this taxing was first made when Cyrenius was governor over Syria. And all went to be taxed, everyone into his own city. And Joseph also went up from Galilee, out of the city of Nazareth, into Judea, unto the City of David, which is called Bethlehem; because he was of the house and lineage of David; to be taxed with Mary his espoused wife, being great with child. And so it was, that while they were there, the days were accomplished that she should be delivered. And she brought forth her firstborn son, and wrapped him in swaddling clothes, and laid him in a manger; because there was no room for them in the inn. And there were in the same country shepherds abiding in the field, keeping watch over their flock by night. And, lo, the angel of the Lord came upon them, and the glory of the Lord shone round about them: and they were sore afraid. And the angel said unto them, Fear not: for behold, I bring you good tidings of great joy, which shall be to all people. For unto you is born this day in the city of David a Saviour, which is Christ the Lord. And this shall be a sign unto you; Ye shall find the babe wrapped in swaddling clothes, lying in a manger. And suddenly there was with the angel a multitude of the heavenly host praising God and saying, Glory to God in the highest, and on earth, peace, good will toward men. And it came to pass, as the angels were gone away from them into heaven, the shepherds said one to another, Let us now go even unto Bethlehem, and see this thing which is come to pass, which the Lord hath made known to us. And they came with haste, and found Mary, and Joseph, and the babe lying in a manger."

Caleb closed the book, and shook his head. Struggling families whose homeland was occupied by enemy soldiers—this he understood.

Then came a voice. "Mary had a baby, yes Lord," Mary sang in a rich alto, clear as a bell and in time with the chair as she rocked baby Joshua.

> "Mary had a baby, yes Lord,
>> The people keep a-comin' an' the train done gone.
> What did she name Him? Yes, Lord;
> What did she name Him? Yes Lord;
>> The people keep a-comin' an' the train done gone.

(The others joined her song.)

She name Him King Jesus, Yes Lord;
She name Him Mighty Couns'lor, Yes Lord;
   The people keep a-comin' an' the train done gone.

Oh where was He borned, Yes, Lord;
   Borned in a manger, Yes Lord;
The people keep a-comin' an' the train done gone."

All that could be heard for the next moments was the creak of the rocking chair.

"Maybe we ain't got it so bad, after all," Abel spoke quietly. "If God done took care of those poor folk an' put His own Son in their care, He can do for us, too." He got up and limped to a corner of the room and brought out a little wooden horse that he had carved for Joshua. He set it down beside the figure of Jesus in the manger. "Joshua can have it when he wakes up. Don't reckon he'll mind it sittin' there for a bit."

Callie brought out a little blue blanket she had crocheted for Joshua and tucked it around him. Then she handed a bundle to Mary.

Mary's beautiful, dark eyes grew wide, then glistened with tears. "Ain't never had a Christmas present befo'."

"I know. Open it."

Mary handed the sleeping baby to Callie and slowly, carefully opened the bundle. It was a calico apron with little pink and blue flowers embroidered on the waist. "It's the best present I ever see. Thank you, Miss Callie." She got up from the chair and tied it on. "I got somethin' fer y'all. I was goin' save it 'til tomorra, but I feels like celebratin' now." They all laughed as she walked to a cabinet in the kitchen and applauded as she pulled out a rich, spicy cider cake.

"Abe, this is for you," Abel handed his son a hand-made knife with a polished wooden handle.

"Thanks, Paw. I got a surprise for you, too." He brought out a bottle of Tennessee whiskey. "I didn't forget."

Caleb took Callie's hand and pulled her off to a corner. "Callie, it's not much, but I figured you know better than anybody what this year's been like. I wanted you to know that wherever you are, you carry my heart with you." He handed her a wooden heart, carved carefully with both their names on it and polished to a gloss. It had a small hole in the top through which was strung a thin, green ribbon to tie around her neck.

Callie giggled a little, "It's beautiful Caleb Maghee! I'll treasure it always! Put it on me." She turned around and lifted her auburn curls, and he carefully tied the ribbon. Smiling, she turned and gave him a hug, then reached in her pocket, took something out, and placed it in the palm of his hand. She giggled again. It was a white stone in the perfect shape of a heart, rubbed slick and clean. "I found it in the creek by the church," she said, "Wherever you are, you can carry my heart with you."

"I love you, Callalily Norton."

Caleb and Callalily walked to town slowly, hand in hand. "In spite of everything, it turned into a good evenin', didn't it," she mused.

Before Caleb could answer, around the corner came three of the soldiers. Two of them had nearly empty whiskey bottles in their hands, and they were alternately arguing and knocking each other down and helping each other up. "Weeellllll, Gentlemen, what do we have here?"

"Looks like that yella boy from up the hill."

Caleb got between Callie and the men and told her, "Keep walking." They quickened their pace.

"His family got a slave up there, too." The men were speaking loudly and fell in behind Caleb and Callie.

One of the other men began to drunkenly sing, "Go down, Moses, way down in Egypt land. Tell ol' Pharaoh, let my people goooooo . . ."

"Hey, Pharaoh!" he was addressing Caleb.

They kept walking, the hecklers following behind. Callie's house was in sight.

"Hey! Yella boy! Don't you know your President has asked you to join us? Oh, he also asked you to let that slave woman go free."

The other man started to sing again.

"Boy! I am a corporal in the Army of the United States of America and I am talkin' to you! Turn around!"

"Run, Callie! Get home!" She raced for her front door as the three soldiers set upon Caleb. He did his best to fight them off, and had it been one-on-one, Caleb could have held his own, but the three men had him on the ground in a moment, kicking him like an animal.

Suddenly, a shot split the air and the three men backed off.

Mr. Norton stood on the porch of his home, rifle in hand. He had fired into the air to frighten the drunken men away;

however, one of the men drew out his pistol and aimed at Mr. Norton. Caleb got to his feet in an instant and ran at the soldier, knocking him off balance. The bullet missed its target and embedded in the pillar of the porch instead of in the man on it.

Realizing their predicament, the three men ran off before the man on the porch decided to aim for them.

Caleb reached Mr. Norton, limping and bleeding badly. "Are you all right, Sir?"

"Yes, I am, but you're a mess. Get in here."

Callie and her mother were horrified by the blood and bruises, and by the near calamity with the guns. They cleaned and bandaged Caleb and tried to convince him to stay the night, but Caleb insisted on leaving. He knew it was unreasonable, but Caleb was embarrassed by the whole scenario. *They say we are immoral and our way of life is wrong, but this is the way they choose to change things*, Caleb thought, *to occupy our town and threaten us and take our livelihood. I cannot support a government that acts in that way*. On the walk home that night, he made a decision to enlist in the Confederate army.

There was no argument that anyone could offer to change Caleb's mind. Abe insisted the farm could not run without his help, and Caleb knew it would be a struggle. Callalily pleaded that her heart was breaking and that she couldn't go on without him, and Caleb knew he would have a hard time without her, as well. Abel offered the most compelling reason not to go: "Are ye goin' te far on yer own brother, Caleb?" For that one he had no answer. He loved Tad, but none of them even knew where Tad was, didn't know if he was still alive. Could he possibly allow the Yanks to overrun the mountain as they had the town, taking what they wanted and killing those who stood in their way? No, he could not, not even for Tad.

Preparation to leave was made quickly. Cold as it was, Caleb picked up his pack one morning, said a tearful good-bye to all, and promised to send back his soldier's pay to be used to run the farm. He also vowed to write down everything in case the papers had need of eye-witness testimony. Then he headed toward Atlanta, the place where he thought he would most quickly realize his goals. When he passed the church with its white-washed exterior that always turned to gray that time of year, he paused for a moment to look out over Big Bear Creek. There was no grass on the hillside. Here and there, remnants of snow and ice dotted the tawny blades left from the summer lawn. Black and brown skeletons of trees clung to the creek's bank. Some, having lost their grip, made precarious bridges over the frozen banks and out into the icy blue water that still bubbled and frothed toward the Tennessee River. A few evergreens dotted the hillside. Yes, there was still some life in this little community and Caleb meant to make sure it survived with the freedom in which it had been born.

Caleb had not gone far when he met two more young men from Angel Head. They were brothers, Thomas and Rayburn Clay. Caleb recognized them from camp meetings. "Where you boys headed?" he asked them.

"Headed to Atlanta to enlist."

"Yanks have taken over ever'thing in Angel Head. We goin' while we can."

"Then we might as well travel together," Caleb said, "but the road may not be the safest way."

Thomas and Rayburn turned out to be good company and very able woodsmen. Their combined knowledge of the outdoors kept them well fed, well rested, and warm most of the time. Water became an issue in the hills. The water that would have fed the freshets along the way was still frozen at higher altitudes, so they were making due with what they could melt of the ice and snow.

One morning, Caleb woke early. The light of dawn was beginning to show through a fog so cold it nearly crackled. Thomas and Rayburn were nowhere in sight. Caleb called to them but there was no answer. After a bit he needed to move around if only to keep warm, so he began to walk. Surely the Clay boys could not be too far away.

Then Caleb saw a warm glow reflecting through the fog. He followed the glow, and came, astonishingly, to a small, rustic cabin. He knocked on the door thinking perhaps he would locate Thomas and Rayburn and some food. A voice invited him in.

Inside the cabin was warm and strange. There was nothing fancy, nothing to indicate a family, but simply a rough-cut table with two chairs, a small cot in a corner with a tan blanket, a huge fireplace with a roaring fire, a small barrel of water, and a potter's wheel, at which sat an elderly man with thick gray eyebrows, an abundant mustache, and a long gray beard, spinning the wheel and molding a mound of wet, rust-colored clay. There were hundreds of gray, brown and rust-colored pots filling the shelves and covering a significant area of the floor. The elderly man motioned for Caleb to sit. He took a black, iron pot from an arm over the fire and a tin from the mantle and commenced to prepare Caleb a cup of tea.

"Thank you, Sir. Any chance there may have been another couple of men here recently?"

*No, no, you're the first person I've seen here in a while. Where you headed, Boy?*

"Headed to Atlanta."

*That's a long trip, dangerous roads.*

"Yes, Sir. That's why we're staying off the main roads. We're going to enlist.

*Soldier?*

"Yes, Sir."

*Look more like a preacher-man.*

"I'm not a preacher, Sir. Funny though, that's what my maw always said," Caleb smiled a little.

The old man had returned to his wheel. As he worked the wheel, he wet his hands and put them to the clay and recited, *Behold, as the clay is in the potter's hand, so are you in my hand. Has not the potter power over the clay to make it what he desires, a vessel for a common purpose or a vessel of honor for a special purpose? You are clay in the hands of the great Potter who wants to prepare you for common service—the kind that is needed consistently and dependably every day, or for a peculiar service—*

*one that may be needed only once, but for a thing very great and honorable.*

Caleb recognized those words! "Who are you?" he asked, and looked up from his tea cup into the startling, emerald green eyes of the old man.

Caleb's eyes opened wide, and he was on the ground under a tree, fog coming in around him. He sat up. Thomas was several feet away and Rayburn was standing guard near the fire. Caleb's heart was beating fast and he was wide awake so he got up and walked to the fire.

"Reckon I'll stand guard now. You can get some sleep," he said to Rayburn, and Rayburn did not argue.

When all three were awake and packed up in the morning and after they had shared their rations and a little chicory coffee made from their meager supply of water, Caleb made a suggestion. "Let's go this way," he said, indicating the direction he had taken in his strange dream.

"Why? That's a little off course," Thomas said.

"Just a hunch I want to check out."

As they got close to where the cabin should be, they heard a welcome sound—running water! Sure enough, instead of the cabin of a potter, Caleb had led them to a moving creek. They drank to their content, then filled up every vessel they had to carry it with them.

"Whosoever drinketh of this water shall thirst again. But whosoever drinketh of the water that I shall give him shall never thirst; but the water that I shall give him shall be in him a well of water springing up into everlasting life," Caleb recited.

"What was that?" Thomas asked.

"Oh, just something I remembered," was all that Caleb would say.

It took more than a week for the three hardy, young men to make their trek. In Atlanta there was commotion everywhere, but since there were also soldiers everywhere, it was not difficult to find the recruiting station. They signed their names and were sent to training briefly, then as a call came for reinforcements, they were marched to western Tennessee.

Life in the camps was not an easy thing. The weather was cold, and even as spring arrived, it was wet and often miserable. Large kettles of beans were prepared every day to fill the stomachs of the men. Caleb and the Clays were also introduced to a thing called "sloosh"—cornmeal and bacon grease made into a cake and wrapped around a ramrod and cooked over the fire. What the cooks called coffee was more often brewed peanuts, potatoes or chicory. Often it was that Caleb daydreamed about his maw's beans, greens and cornbread! He also daydreamed about Callie, but he never dwelt on those daydreams much because they made his heart ache. Daily Caleb continued to keep a detailed and accurate record in his journal of all that was taking place.

Near the tracks of the Nashville and Chattanooga Railroad, the soldiers were placed under the command of General Albert Sidney Johnston. Johnston marched them south to Decatur, then turned toward Corinth, Mississippi where they intended to amass additional troops under the respective commands of Generals Bragg, Ruggles and Beauregard. By then, it was April.

# The Battle of Shiloh

April 1862: The weather was lovely, still a little wet from all the rain that had fallen, but warming. The sun beamed, and it seemed that overnight, its yellow rays had coaxed little shoots out of the ground and tiny buds onto the trees. Something was afoot in the Johnston camp. Word had come that only twenty-two miles away at Pittsburg Landing on the Tennessee River, Ulysses S. Grant had dug in with his fifty-thousand men. In addition, he had no knowledge of Johnston's presence.

"We can surprise 'em!" Johnston pushed, but we have to move fast. The troops moved out immediately in the attempt to cover the distance between themselves and the enemy, taking little time to break for meals and little time for rest.

The morning of April 6 dawned clear as men clad in gray and brown and marching under the flag of the Confederacy approached the Federal camps. A small skirmish arose as they encountered a reconnaissance along the Corinth road, but Johnston's men were too close to give the Federals any advantage from discovery.

Some of the Southerners were chomping at the bit to get to fight, but there were many like Caleb who had not yet seen combat and who could feel every nerve on edge. Finally, at nine-thirty, as the sun looked down over the hills, the order was given to the whole army to advance. In the Union camps, men were shocked to attention by the sound of gunfire. There was nothing to do but get out of the way, and they did that fast, returning a few shots, but causing little damage.

Reaching the first Union camp and finding it deserted, the hungry Confederates ransacked tents, knapsacks and abandoned cooking pots for something to fill their bellies, but before long the order was called, "Fix bayonets!" The focus returned to the fight and onward surged the tsunami of gray. From somewhere, a blood chilling yell began. It spread from man to man, each releasing his pent-up energy and fear through his vocal folds and splitting the air. "They fly!" was heard, and encouraged, the Confederates pressed forward.

At Pittsburg Landing, Grant was taken by surprise. He had been biding his time following General Halleck's orders to wait for Buell's Army of the Ohio before proceeding south. Tad, however, was not surprised. Stitch had been acting strangely restless all night, pacing back and forth and whining. Tad and those with him were ready to advance, but no order came. When the orders were finally given, they were for defense instead of offense and Tad, Stitch and the Federals rose to whatever challenge may come.

By the middle of the morning, it looked as though Johnston's tactic would work. One Union frontline after another fell to the relentless Confederates. The fight moved uphill around the small church, and the armies from the North had no intention of giving up. Casualties mounted on both sides and the battle seemed far from over.

The sun rose higher in the sky, and General Grant sent an order to hold the hilltop "at all hazards." Undergrowth and blackberry bushes that the Federals named the "hornet's nest" made it difficult for the Confederates to charge up the hill and to hold their lines. Tad stood with the men on top of the hill, aiming to stop the advance. Ping! Pain like a hot knife stabbed into Tad's left shoulder. "I'm alright," he told himself. "I can still shoot." And he did, not realizing he shot in the direction of his own brother.

\* \* \*

The woods at the foot of Shiloh Church hill received a barrage of artillery rounds. Trees were cut down to twigs and sparks caught the woods on fire sending thick smoke into the midst of the attack. Caleb tried to escape it, but he could not seem to get away from that smoke, no matter how hard he tried. It hurt his eyes and blinded him; it filled his lungs and made it hard to breathe. After a while, all he could think of was to get to water. "There is a pond," he said to himself, "close to that orchard."

\* \* \*

In the orchard, peach blossoms were in full bloom and ironically lovely in the midst of the carnage. A group of Confederate soldiers took refuge under those trees, only to be set upon by General William Tecumseh Sherman and his troops. Men were cut down and the peach blossoms fell down upon them like snow. A courageous man, a camp follower attached to Sherman's troops, had volunteered to deliver a vital message. Assignment completed, he ducked behind the trunk of a peach tree and prayed, "Lawd, somehow use this that Your will be done. Don't let all these men die in vain." That man's name was Jobie, and he had taken the last name *Maghee*.

\* \* \*

Tad, still on the hill in the heat of battle, suddenly felt very light-headed. He was chilled on his left side, and touched his shirt to find it soaked with blood. He reached for his canteen as dark clouds rolled before his eyes and he staggered. There was a bullet hole in the canteen. "Stitch," he said, "get me to water." He took hold of Stitch's collar and they moved forward slowly and cautiously through the rage of the battle toward a small pond near the peach orchard.

Suddenly, Tad heard someone calling his name. It was Jobie! "Stitch! Take me to Jobie!" Stitch continued to lead him on until they met their friend.

Artillery rounds blazed through the air and Jobie had to shout to be heard. "You bleedin', Tad; you bleedin' bad." He could not hide the concern in his voice.

"I just need some water, that's all."

"C'mon then." Jobie put an arm around Tad to support him, and he and Stitch guided Tad to the pond, but before he could bend over to drink, through the smoke he saw another familiar figure.

"Turtle!" Tad called, hoping he was not hallucinating. "Turtle! Over here! Turtle!"

Caleb looked in the direction of the voice. There was no mistaking it! "Tad! I'm here!" he shouted. As he stood peering into the smoke, a bullet cut through the air and grazed Caleb's temple. He tried to steady himself, then fell face down into the pond. His mind realized that he could not breathe, but he couldn't make his body do anything to correct it.

"No!" Tad cried out and pulled away from the horrified Jobie. Stitch barked behind him, but Tad pushed away through the shallow, muddy pond, around and across other men who had come to this place seeking, as he had, relief from the battle. Some of the men wore blue and some of the men wore gray; some were dead and some still clutched with all their strength for one more breath.

Tad reached his brother and pulled his head up out of the water. He wondered why Turtle felt so heavy. "Turtle, I'm sorry! I didn't mean it when I said I wasn't your brother . . . I'm sorry I was jealous . . ."

Caleb coughed. "Are you real?" he asked, his voice husky.

Tad laughed a strange, choking guffaw.

Caleb hugged his brother. "Tad, you'll always be my brother, no matter what you say."

"Turtle, I'm hurt purty bad. Promise me something."

"Sure, Tad, anything."

"Tell Paw and Grampaw and little Joshua I love 'em."

167

"You can tell 'em, Tad. You're gonna be fine."

Tad was beginning to shake. He felt awfully cold. "Jobie and Stitch are here. Git 'em home."

"I will." Caleb's eyes filled with tears. "We will."

"And you gotta remember . . ." Tad's eyes closed.

"What?" Caleb shook his brother desperately. He felt very weak. "Remember what?"

Tad came around and he looked very purposefully into Caleb's eyes, "'Carry my tears.'"

"But I don't know how. I don't know what it means."

"Love people, Turtle. Love 'em like Jesus done. Love 'til it hurts. Teach 'em to love each other that way. It's the only way fer folks to heal. I know that now. It's the only way fer our nation to heal. I wish I could go with you, Turtle. Don't forget. Do it for both of us."

Tad felt his energy leaving him. Then a strong hand reached down and firmly pulled him to his feet. "Companion!" He looked into those incredible eyes and felt his strength return.

*Come, enter into the joy of my Father!*

Tad walked beside Companion, and it seemed to him that they walked on top of the water. The smoke and the battle were gone, and so was the pain in his shoulder. They stood together for a moment on a peaceful, green hillside under warm, golden light, overlooking a crystal clear river bordered by magnificent, strange, fruit-laden trees. A woman clothed in a white robe stood on the bank waving to him. He recognized her!

"Maw!" He waved back and ran down the hill to her. "Maw! I'm home!"

* * *

When Jobie reached the brothers, they still clung to one another, eyes closed. He knelt next to them with Stitch by his side. Caleb's face was streaked with blood but he was breathing. Tad was not. Jobie picked up Caleb first and carried him to a dry place and instructed Stitch, "Don't you leave 'im, Boy."

Stitch licked Jobie's hand, then lay down beside Caleb.

Jobie returned to the water and lifted Tad's body. He carried his more-than-friend back to the Union line, and even though he didn't think about it then, he later realized that no one fired a shot in their direction. When he reached a place of safety, he placed Tad with the Union dead and arranged his limbs so he looked comfortable. The eyes of his fellow soldiers spoke the question. "That ma brother," was all Jobie answered. As he looked one last time at the face of Jacob "Tad" Maghee, he had the distinct impression that the brother he loved was somewhere else entirely and that he was healed and happy.

# The Way Back

Caleb woke up on a cot in a plantation house that had been badly damaged by cannon fire and then taken over as a field hospital where he was being treated for his wounds. The little, white, heart-shaped stone was still in his pocket but his journal was gone. Stitch was beside his cot. As soon as he saw the dog, he remembered everything.

"You were found after the battle with this here dog watchin' over ye like a guardian angel," he was told, but no one could answer any questions about how he came to be where he was or what happened to his brother.

Caleb's body healed quickly, which was more than could be said for the other soldiers in that make-shift hospital. Some had lost limbs during the fighting; some had lost sight in their eyes; many had lost hope, and that was the worst thing of all. In the midst of their groans, Caleb heard his brother's last request, words that he had quoted from a time past: "Carry my tears."

He began to go around and talk to the other soldiers, offering what small words of encouragement he could think of. Stitch was a great help and sometimes got the wounded men to smile. Then a thought occurred to Caleb and he requested paper and ink. He began to write letters home as the soldiers dictated, and it seemed as they thought about their homes, their pain lessened a bit.

One day word arrived for Caleb. The corporal delivering the message carried Caleb's journal. He spoke briefly with the doctor who looked at the journal, then walked directly to Caleb.

"Caleb, it seems you have been called to Richmond," the doctor told him. "President Davis is in need of war correspondents, and someone to help him write his book. One of the men who was with you at Corinth found your journal and sent it off to the president thinking he would find it fascinating and insightful reading. President Davis believes you to be the man he needs."

Caleb and Stitch left with the corporal that very day. In Richmond, he was introduced to President Jefferson Davis who put him to work immediately writing vital instructions to his generals and also helping him to gather notes to begin his book. Caleb remained in Richmond, but in his heart he had already begun to travel home. On the morning of April 3, 1865, Caleb was summoned urgently to the president's office with the others who had faithfully served the often difficult man who ran the Confederate States, and where that same man dismissed them to wherever they might find safety.

"We're going home, Stitch." Stitch wagged his tail.

As they walked, they met others who were headed home, some not knowing whether they would even find "home" still there. Some bore injuries that would make their lives difficult for as long as they continued to draw breath. Stories of Gettysburg, tales of Grant and Lee at Appomattox Court House, and rumors of the death of President Lincoln reached Caleb by word of mouth. In a small town through which he walked, he glimpsed a newspaper with the headline "Lincoln Shot." When finally he arrived in Tennessee, he found the war-torn landscape of his beloved state, burned, and pitted, trees cut down to twigs by cannon-fire, crops ravaged. His heart grieved for his country that was going to have to find a way to heal. He feared it would be a long process.

Then on a day when the golden sun beamed warm on the land, Caleb and Stitch came to the Tennessee River. They could hear it even before they saw its silver-blue flood that splashed and gurgled and washed the land it crossed with hope and with promise. The two pushed on and did not rest until the river forked and received Big Bear Creek. There, Caleb stripped down and he and Stitch launched out into the water, spirits floating free as the foam on the current. Somehow it seemed the banks of the creek had escaped the scorch of the rest of the land. The water rushed along, pure, clear, and free between the greening trees, and in its depths Caleb felt clean for the first time in years.

Home was less than an hour away. Caleb wondered what changes he would find. Certainly, some things could never be the same. In his mind, Caleb saw Tad as he last saw him, his brown eyes so intense. He heard his last words: "Carry my tears. Love people, Turtle. Love 'em like Jesus done. Love 'til it hurts. Teach 'em to love each other that way. Don't forget. Do it for both of us."

"I'll do my best, Tadpole. I sure will do my best."

Caleb climbed the steep trail without difficulty, but Stitch, recognizing where he was, bounded ahead. Everything—the yellow and purple wildflowers by the wayside, the sound of the breeze through those particular poplars and firs, the smell of the mountain air—was familiar and spoke "Welcome home!" to his heart. He walked around the lake and stopped to look for a moment, remembering a summer day swimming with Tad— he was still Jacob then—and he could almost feel a tiny snapping turtle clenched on his toe. He smiled.

Up the hill, a slightly bent figure of an elderly man rounded the barn. Stitch nearly knocked him over. "Stitch?" The man petted the dog, then raised up to squint his eyes and peer down the sunny hill hopefully, then certainly. "Caleb!"

"Grampaw!" With the abandon of a child, Caleb ran the rest of the way, and by the time he reached the top of the hill, his grandfather, his father, Mary, little Joshua and his beautiful Callalily all surrounded him with hugs and words of welcome. "I'm home!"

* * *

After dinner one evening shortly after his return, Caleb looked out and spotted his father alone on the rock down by the lake. He walked down to join him. There was something he had to say.

"Paw, I was there at the end, with Tad."

"Were you, Son?"

"Yes, Sir. He said to tell you and Grampaw and Joshua that he loves you."

Abe silently nodded his head.

"And there is something else."

"What's that then?"

"Jobie was with him, too. And Stitch, of course."

"Ain't even a grave where we can go visit him. But I'm glad y'all were with him. I'm glad . . . he weren't alone."

* * *

For the first time since 1860, the fair was held again at Big Bear Creek. Many of the events were the same as they had always been—quilting, canning, baking, livestock, and the "big buck." There were horse shoes to toss and arrows to shoot and amazingly, considering the devastation of the war, there was abundant food to enjoy. However, one new event was scheduled and everyone around was invited to participate— the wedding of Callalily Norton to Caleb Maghee!

The perfect autumn day arrived with a warm, golden sun shining on red, orange and yellow leaves under a flawless azure sky. Abel stood at the lectern of the packed Big Bear Creek Church while Caleb, attended by his father and dressed in a new suit and his grandfather's hand-me-down tie, stood awaiting his bride. The two camp meeting fiddle players were, for the day, "violinists," and softly played a relatively new piece called "Wedding March," by Felix Mendelssohn. Slowly down the aisle of the church walked Petunia, Laurel, Daisy, and Rose, each carrying a bouquet of purple, yellow and pink wild flowers. Callalily followed in a snow-white dress and lace veil, carrying a bouquet of pale pink rhododendron blossoms. She held the arm of her father as she walked toward Caleb. At the front of the church, Grayson Norton placed his eldest daughter's hand in Caleb's and smiled, but there were tears welling up in his eyes.

Caleb looked into the happy face of his bride, and for just a moment he thought about that day he had proposed to her for the first time. "Callalily Norton, will you pledge to marry me whenever I can afford to take you as my wife? Good! I'll talk to you later!" Then he had slapped the ring into the palm of her hand and kissed her hard and run off with Tad. He wished Tad was there, and Maw. And then he was back in the present, gazing into the unbelievably blue eyes of his beloved and declaring with all his overflowing heart, "I do."

After the ceremony, the whole community joined in the celebration. There was cake and punch and food for all. Glasses were lifted to the couple and their future. Gifts were presented. Among the gifts was a shiny wooden box that contained the silver flatware that Caleb's grandparents had passed to Alice and Abe on their wedding day. Tradition, Caleb decided, is a very happy thing. At one point during the reception, the church elders called Caleb away for a moment. They had an important question to ask him.

When they got back home that evening, Caleb said, "Callie, I have something to discuss with you. Do you remember how I always wanted to go off to the big city to write for a newspaper and bring the news to the people?"

"Yes, my love," Callalily responded, snuggling up to him and not really in the mood for conversation at that moment.

"Well, I studied it through for a long time and I came to the conclusion that the best news I could possibly bring to the people was the news of the Gospel. What do you think?"

"What do I think about what, Darlin'?" she asked as she kissed his neck.

"About me being the preacher at Big Bear Creek Church. I could work here on the farm and still be close enough to the church to preach every Sunday. 'Course there would be other duties as well . . ."

"Caleb . . ."

". . . but I'm sure I can make the time for them . . ."

"Honey . . ."

". . . and the elders really want me to consider . . ."

"CALEB!"

"What?"

"We'll talk about it in the morning."

"Oh . . ."

\* \* \*

Life was good on Big Bear Mountain. Caleb enjoyed working the land with his father and grandfather as they once had.

Joshua and Stitch became the best of friends. Callie and Mary worked together as they had for years, keeping the place, and the men, in order. There was laughter in the Maghee home once again.

Caleb did become the pastor of the Big Bear Creek Church, and the whole community was glad. Even Brother Edwards agreed that it was a perfect fit. Very often Caleb encouraged the congregation to carry the tears of the Master, to love one another, especially those who were returning from the war, regardless of the side on which they had fought.

"Remember the words of instruction," he often exhorted the people, "'If my people, which are called by my name, shall humble themselves, and pray, and seek my face, and turn from their wicked ways, then will I hear from heaven, and will forgive their sin, and will heal their land.'" It was not in a newspaper, but it was the news the people needed, and Sunday after Sunday the church was filled. As his reputation grew, Caleb was asked to travel to preach camp meetings in other places and he gladly obliged. It was not only to the pulpit that Caleb carried the tears of the Master, either. If anyone needed help, Caleb was soon on the scene.

* * *

In the spring, as he had vowed to do, Jobie climbed Big Bear Mountain once again to the place that he considered home. Caleb saw him on the lake path and sent little Joshua up to the house to tell Callie and Mary that company was coming. Then rushed to meet Jobie. Of course, Stitch beat him to the greeting and had already licked his hands and face before Caleb arrived. The two men clasped hands in an enthusiastic shake that turned into a hug.

"There's ma big brother!" Jobie grinned. "It's beautiful, just like I remembers it. And you lookin' all growed up!"

"Jobie, you wouldn't believe it! I married Callalily and became a preacher!"

"Haha, yo' maw always said so!"

"Yes, she did. Wonder how she knew. But come on up to the house. The women probably have half the storehouse laid out on the table for you."

"That's good news! My stomach's a-gnawin' at ma backbone, hehe."

They opened the door and walked into the keeping room. Caleb announced, "Look who it is!"

Callie ran over to greet Jobie, but stopped short when she saw the look on his face. He was staring at Mary, eyes big and hands trembling. "Mama?" he asked in an odd, almost frightened voice.

"Sit him down, Caleb," Callie said. "Mary, get him some water."

Mary was understandably uneasy at the reaction of this stranger. She got the water and Jobie drank it down.

"Your name Mary, girl?"

"Yes."

"How you came here?"

Mary ran out of the house and Callie followed.

At that moment Abe and Able came in. "Jobie! Welcome home, Son!"

"Paw, something's wrong."

"That girl, Mary," Jobie asked, "where she come from?"

Abe did not fully understand. "Jobie, she's not a slave. Now it's true, I took money to her family and brought her back here to help with everything when Alice died, and I wanted to make it look like she was a slave so's things didn't happen like they happened with you, but she's a free woman an' she knows it. She just ain't suppose' to tell anybody. After what happened to you and Paw . . . Jobie?"

Jobie was regaining his wits. He told the story that years before he had told Tad in the hay loft, how his family had started out with a mother, father, six brothers and two sisters, and how they were sold off one by one.

"One night Mama wake me up an' tell me we leavin' and be real quiet. We took off out behind the house and kep' on goin' all night. When daylight come, we hid in the woods. We keep on like that fo' days; then Mary start to git sick. Mama did all she knowed to do but Mary kep' on cryin' an' a group of men find us. Mama say to me, 'Run, boy,' so I run, and then I heared a shot behind me. Mama was dade, but Mary were alive. She weren't cryin' no more, but she look kindly funny. I pick up Mary and sit beside Mama, an' then I fell asleep. When I wake up, a man standin' there, a man with green eyes, an' he tell me he goin' take me to a place where it safe. He look at Mary and touch her real gentle, and she smile and fall asleep. Then he say somethin' strange. He say, 'Carry my tears.' So I picks up Mary and follows that man. We walk a long way, and then we come to a ol' church, and they's singin' comin' out that church. We walks in an' a man and woman comes up to me and I hands Mary to 'em an' I says, 'Her name Mary.' I never see her again . . . 'til now."

"She was living with a family in Angel Head," Abe offered the missing piece of the puzzle. "She wasn't their slave. They were raising her free, but they had hard times and I said I would pay them a year of her wages and she could come work for my family for room and board the first year. Then I'd pay her wages after that. You can ask her. She's a free woman."

"She growed up to look just like our mama—so beautiful."

"Carry my tears," Caleb repeated.

"That's what he say. I think I scared her. I didn't mean to scare her."

Mary was sent for and the story was told again. She listened with eyes shining like pearls. "Then you ma brother?"

"'Pears so."

What a wonderful reunion took place on Big Bear Mountain that day! They ate, drank, sang, laughed and cried until time for bed.

"Yer welcome to our room while yer here, Jobie," Callie offered.

"Thank ya, Miss Callie, but I reckon I'll go up to the hay lof', if it's all the same."

The next morning at breakfast, they laughed about that decision. "I thinks the mice done took over ma house."

"Will you be moving back, Jobie? We'd be proud to have you. We'll even evict the mice," Abel teased.

"Thank you, very kind, but I'm jus' here to visit before I head to Indiana."

"Tarnation! What's in Indianny?"

I met a man after the war ended. He tell me they's orphans from all over the South, orphans 'cause the war. They put 'em on trains—orphan trains they calls 'em—and sends 'em out West to be adopted. Sometimes that works for the white chil'ren, but mos' the time white and Negro chil'ren jus' took for slaves. They ain't no better off than they was befo'. We decide we gonna go to Indiana and purchase some land and build a house out there an' take on some o' those orphans, give 'em a home, teach 'em. I gots five hundred Federal dollars from ma army pay. They finally let me enlist in July a' '62 an' I saved all I could. That man an' me gonna put our money together to give those babies a chance in this worl'.

"I'd like to come with you." Heads turned. It was Mary. "I saved ma money, too. Reckon two mens might need a woman if yo' goin take up raisin' orphans."

"Mary!"

"Not that I'm unhappy here, mind, but I reckon ma brother need me. Them orphan babies need me."

"'Carry my tears,' Mary. I think the Master is calling you, too," Caleb said, amazed at how some things in life work out. Who would have believed that Jobie would find his sister in his very own house?

181

Caleb continued to work on the farm and preach in the church for the rest of his life. He and Callie helped to raise Joshua and had two boys of their own. They named them Tad and Abel, and when they grew up, they continued to run the farm on Big Bear Mountain.

The name of Caleb Maghee became well known in the hills of Tennessee. People said when he talked about the Lord, it was as if he had walked with Him personally. If Caleb could comfort a bereaved family, share his bread with someone in need, help a man get a mule cart out of a ditch, or offer anyone a word of encouragement, he did so. He did his best each day to carry his Master's tears, and hundreds of people glimpsed Jesus in his eyes.

# Epilogue

April 1930: Caleb Maghee stood in the family cemetery on the hill above his house. It was becoming harder and harder for him to climb that hill, but it comforted him to be there with his maw, paw, grandparents, Stitch, and his beloved Callie. The cemetery was his favorite place to pray and to prepare his sermons away from the bustle of the farm and the chaos of his great-grandchildren who adored him and always wanted to be in his lap. It was easy there to listen.

Sunset had come and gone in a blaze of orange, pink and purple, and the mist rose from valley to mountaintop, blending the horizon into the darkening sky. Still, Caleb remained. He walked over to a simple stone that did not mark a grave, but a memory. On it was carved the name *Jacob "Tad" Maghee, April 6, 1862*. He knelt down and touched the stone. As he did he remembered the words of Emmanuel Potter:

"Has not the potter power over the clay to make it what he desires, a vessel for a common purpose or a vessel of honor for a special purpose? You are clay in the hands of the great Potter who wants to prepare you for common service—the kind that is needed consistently and dependably every day, and which sometimes goes unnoticed or is taken for granted, or for a peculiar service—one that may be needed only once, but for a thing very great and honorable. Both different; both necessary."

"I am the common vessel," Caleb spoke to the memory of his brother. "You were the vessel of honor."

Caleb stood, and the stars began to emerge one by one, and an ambiguous glow in the fog burst forth as a brilliant full moon.

"The heavens are telling the glory of God; and the firmament showeth his handiwork," he quoted aloud.

Caleb thought he felt a hand on his arm, and he thought he heard his mother's voice whisper in his ear: "My little preacher-man."

"I'm not a preacher-man," he answered. Then he heard her laughter, light and joyous on the mountain breeze, and he smiled.

# Verses Cited

(Scripture references based on the King James Version)

*Also from Beverly R. Green*

# CARRY MY TEARS

### A MYTH

## Beverly R. Green

"This book was one that I could not put down until I had finished it."
—Rosemary Cook Davis

www.ichthuspublications.com

25529431R00104

Made in the USA
Columbia, SC
04 September 2018